ANGEL'S TRAITOR

WINGS OF DECEIT

BOOK 3

SUSAN HARRIS

ANGEL'S TRAITOR
Copyright ©2024 Susan Harris
All rights reserved.

ISBN: **978-1-63422-573-1** (paperback)
ISBN: **978-1-63422-548-9** (e-book)
Cover Design by: Gem Promotions
Typography by: Gem Promotions
Proofing by: Ashley Brilinski

APPENDIX OF
CHARACTERS & NAMES

ANGELS:

<u>The Imperium of the Angels:</u>
    Rieka – RIY-KAH

<u>League of Dominious: Warrior Angels</u>
    Nathaniel – Na-Than-yal
    Abraxas – Ab-Brak-Sus
    Devika – Day-vee-ka
    Verena – Ver-ray-nah
    Cassiopeia – Cass-ee-O-pee-uh
    Adriel – Ad-ree-el
    Adair – Ay-Dare
    Saskia – Sahs-kee-ah
    Draegan –Dray-Gan
    Asterin – As-ter-in
    Makata – Maka-ta

<u>Seraphan: Disgraced Angels:</u>
    Ascian – As-ci-an
    Cadoc – Ca-doc

APPENDIX OF CHARACTERS AND NAMES:

Takara – Ta-Ka-ra
Khione – Key-own-knee
Raisel – Ray-zel
Niran – Knee-ran

<u>Non- warrior Angels:</u>
Kalila – Kay-lee-la
Eliseo – El-ee-say-oh
Hannele – Han-ne-le
Aramis – A-Ruh-Mis

<u>Other Angel's</u>
Zadkiel - Zad-kiel
Akora - Ako-ra

HUMANS:

<u>Rebels:</u>
Raven Cassidy – Ray-Vin Kas-Uh-Dee
Hayes Kennedy – Haze Ken-id-e
Tiernan Byrne – Tear-Nan Burn
James - James
Niamh – Knee-of
Aoife – Eee-Fa
Donnacha – Done-ick-a
Róisín – Row-Sheen

Be careful who you trust,
Even the devil used to be an angel.
Unknown

CHAPTER
ONE

I couldn't fucking die today.

I could not die today because a vapid, sparkly bitch had dropped me from the sky to face-plant onto the cold hard ground and left me to either die from my injuries, or be eaten by wastelanders.

I was too fucking stubborn to let Saskia, of all angels, be the one who ended my life.

Not that I had ever expected my death to be anything but bloody, however, I would be damned if I had evaded death this long only to be killed by a raging bitch with jealousy issues. If I somehow managed to survive the fall, I was going to kill her, slowly, and enjoy every bloody minute of it.

Wind whipped around me, the speed of my descent making it nearly impossible to prepare my body for the fall, and the burn between my shoulder blades made me cry out, the sound swallowed by the rush of wind. The ground came looming into view, and a spike of fear

3

coursed through me as the inevitability of crashing really sunk in.

"Let's see just how durable you actually are, human. If the fall doesn't kill you, then the cannibal bastards will."

I was moments away from landing in one of the most dangerous caverns the wastelanders inhabited. In the caverns in the broken M8 motorway, just on the border of where Cork and Limerick used to meet, where angels had fought one another and ripped the roads to pieces, lived the biggest number and most vicious of the wastelanders. It was here that Rebels were thrown, and forced to prove they could fight well enough to be worthy of being called a soldier.

The ground was suddenly rushing up to meet me as I plunged into the cavern. Curling myself into a ball to try and minimize the damage to my body, and give myself a fighting fucking chance, I still hit the ground hard, my left arm and side taking most of the impact. Biting down hard enough on the inside of my mouth to stop the scream that was trying to claw its way out of my throat, I tasted my own blood as I swallowed.

Pain ricocheted through my body, my arm howling with a fresh agony that told me I'd dislocated it. Again. This was not the first time that I'd dislocated my shoulder. It always hurt like a bitch. I tried to calm the rapid beating of my heart as I took in a breath, and holy fuck that hurt too. I probably had a broken rib or three considering the rattle in my chest when I tried to breathe.

Pulling myself into a sitting position, I leaned against

the wall, closing my eyes, and taking a minute to appreciate the fact that I wasn't dead, even if the pain kinda made me wish I was. But I had taken worse beatings before and survived. Pain was irrelevant and a trapping of your mind. I can overcome a little pain.

Opening my eyes again, I scanned my surroundings. I was sitting in a cold, damp, and dark corner of the cavern, with walls surrounding me on three sides, and only one way in and one way out, deeper into the cavern. That was good. I would only have to keep an eye on one place that the cannibal bastards would come for me. Glancing upward, I saw how far into the wastelanders' territory I had fallen. I would need two arms in order to climb back up and right now, my left arm felt like it would rather not do any climbing if we could help it at all, so I had no choice but to walk straight into more danger.

In the distance, I could hear the shrieking and the growling from the creatures, and knew I'd have to get my ass moving or become dinner. Lifting my right hand up to my pounding head, I winced at the pain and brought my hand down and looked down at my fingers. Blood.

Fuck. This was not good. I might have been able to try and call my power to me, and sneak past the wastelanders even injured as I was, but there was no doubt the scent of my blood would bring the wastelanders right to me, and I had one banjaxed arm and no weapon.

I shifted in my sitting position, jostling my arm, hissing out at the sting of pain as tears blurred my vision. I was tired of fighting. I was so damn tired of war and blood and pain, and I wanted it to end. I wished that I could close my eyes and when I woke up, this entire life I'd lived had been one big nightmare.

The tears spilled out and cascaded down my face.

"Raven, get up. You fight until you are dead and cannot fight. Saskia does not get to be the one who put you in a grave. Get up and fight!"

The sound of Adriel's voice in my head was enough to stop the flow of tears. If he saw me here, wallowing, letting the pain make me weak, Adriel would be so disappointed in me. I was a fighter; a survivor, and Saskia wasn't gonna be the catalyst that got me killed.

Getting to my feet as easily as I could, I tried to assess the injuries I'd gotten in the fall. Most of it I could deal with, but my arm was a liability and I needed both arms in order to try and get out of here. Back in training, we were shown how to dislocate and relocate shoulders, hands, and fingers in order to escape captivity, or at least to fix it enough so that it was less of an impediment.

This was gonna hurt like a bitch and I knew I would pay for it later. If I popped it back into place and it didn't go back quite like it should, then I'd have to suffer it being dislocated again. I'd deal with those consequences if I managed to get myself out alive.

For fuck sake...I had to be running out of lives by now, right?

Backing against the wall, I angled by body and ran at full speed, slamming myself against the other wall so as to force the shoulder back into place. Firey pain splintered down my arm, and I let loose a cry, then vomited on the ground from the wave of nausea that made my legs buckle.

It hadn't worked.

I steeled my resolve, walked gingerly back against the cavern and took a moment. Then I rushed toward the wall again, slamming harder against it, and was rewarded when I heard the resounding sound of a pop, and the worst of the pain eased. I placed a hand on my stomach, taking in some air, ignoring the way my chest ached. Rotating my shoulder, I felt the sting of pain, but it was bearable.

Cocking my head because it was suddenly very quiet all around me, I noted that I couldn't hear the shrieks and the growls from the distance. There was this eerie lull of silence before I heard the shrieks again, closer this time.

They knew there was fresh meat in their territory.

This was bad. This was really bad.

I grabbed the end of my t-shirt, wishing I had the jacket Adriel had given me to help block out the sudden coldness I felt as I wiped the blood from my face. It wouldn't help, having my clothes smelling of blood, but it gave me time to rally my thoughts, and prepare myself for battle.

If I stayed here, in this confined space, I could be overrun depending on how many wastelanders happened to come looking for dinner. My power would be useless in the long run, once they got a whiff of fresh blood, but for now, if I could hold it, it might get me far enough to pick up a weapon along the way.

I slipped out of the relative safety of the cavern, making my way down a dark tunnel. I was grateful then for that sliver of angelic DNA that made my eyesight better than a human's as my eyes quickly adjusted to the darkness. It was a narrow tunnel that seemed to go on for ages, and then it branched off into other tunnels, and gave me no indication which way might be the best way forward.

Straight ahead, I heard shrieks and growls, so going that way would be suicidal even if it was the right answer. I could hear the wheeze in my chest, and felt the ache in my shoulder, but I concentrated as much as possible and called my power to me. It protested to begin with, and then it washed over me in a sudden burst that had me sucking in a breath.

I headed down one of the quieter tunnels, the scent of blood and flesh smacking into me and as nauseous as I was from the pain, bile was creeping up my throat. Forcing it down, I slowly made my way down the tunnel. A low snarl had me flattening myself against the wall as a wastelander came out of nowhere, his nose in the air as he sniffed.

Making myself look at him, I noted he was missing both ears, and part of his cheek, like something had bitten them right off. His hair and face were caked in blood, and I was glad the fucker was missing his ears so he couldn't hear the way my heart was beating against my chest like a war drum. His ripped clothing hung off him in rags, revealing jagged bones protruding from his skin, his stomach hollow, and as he walked, you could hear the creak of his bones.

The creature sniffed the air again, let out a pained whine, then whipped around to look directly at me. For a moment, I thought he could see me, dead eyes seeming to lock with mine as he sniffed again, but then he roared in my face with frustration.

The smell of his rancid breath nearly undid me.

The feel of something running over my boots had me looking down, a rat skuttling down the tunnel. The wastelander shrieked, the sound making the hairs on the back of my neck stand to attention and I watched as the creature lunged, grabbed the rat, and brought it right to his jagged teeth, biting into the live rodent with a sickening crunch, fresh blood spraying his face.

Before I could think too much on it, I slowly started making my way further down the tunnel, conscious of the sounds of movement behind me in the distance. I could see a little more light a ways down, and I hoped that meant an easier ascent.

The tunnel opened and I stepped out into an area the size of a football pitch. It was a graveyard. The skeletal remains of those who had no doubt been eaten by the wastelanders littered the way, the bones literally ripped apart, and I could only imagine the wastelanders tearing flesh and bone from their victims to get as much meat as possible.

I tried not to focus on the bones, I tried to not glance down at all as I made my way across this field of death, but my steps faltered and when I looked down I spotted the carcass of what must have been a very small child. I assumed this, because there was a very small teddy bear close to the skeleton's skull, but I wasn't sure what colour the bear used to be, because it was now covered in caked blood.

How many of these bones belonged to humans who had been broken by the angels and tossed here to be eaten? All evidence of the angel's depravity gone with no trace. I thought of Matthew, Noelle's brother, and how the angels had left him to be found broken and eaten. How many families had come here, in search of signs of their loved ones?

These people were the real victims of the war between angels and humans, the ones who couldn't protect themselves and the Rebels couldn't protect either. I would never erase the image of this place from my mind for as long as I lived.

Stepping back, I heard something crunch under my feet, and realized that I had stepped back onto a brittle bone. The sound of it snapping under my feet echoed through the field. I braced myself for an attack, was almost relieved when none came but that was when I noticed all the movement in my peripheral vision.

One by one, I watched as about ten wastelanders stepped onto the field from different directions, effectively pinning me in. My power was still wrapped around me, but they were looking right in my direction. I felt something sliding down my face, realized the cut to my face was bleeding again, and I knew I was done for.

They advanced, snarling and snapping their teeth,

sniffing the air to pinpoint my location. I knew that the chances of me getting out of here intact were slim, even slimmer if I couldn't find a weapon to use against them. They would tear me to pieces, and no one would ever know that Saskia was to blame.

I felt a presence behind me, felt warm breath against the back of my neck. I reacted out of sheer instinct, kicking up a shard of bone and when it was in my grasp, I spun, shoving the shard into the creature's eye socket. It screamed as I yanked the shard out, then I plunged it into his throat. Blood poured as it grabbed at the shard, pulling it out and then dropping down to the ground, gurgling and jerking until the thing died.

One of the other wastelanders looked at the body on the ground and immediately went over and started to peel the rotten flesh from the bones. Two more wastelanders joined him, and then they started fighting over the unexpected meal, snapping their teeth at each other.

I whirled round, weaving through the bone graveyard looking for an escape route. The other wastelanders were now distracted by their deceased friend, and I could tell they weren't as devolved mentally as some of the wastelanders. They moved like a unit, like they had done this before, stalked prey and backed it into a corner.

But I wasn't just any fucking prey.

I was Raven Cassidy.

I was not gonna die today.

Ignoring the burn in my chest, as I scanned the bones and almost let out a cry of relief as I spotted something I could use as a weapon. Weighing up the pros and cons of giving my location away, I pushed aside what used to be someone's chest cavity and picked up the hurley. The wood was speckled with blood, but I had seen the lads playing hurling in the fields by the barracks, and I knew that if you got hit hard enough with the ash stick, it would hurt like hell.

I gave myself a second to steady myself and then I let go of the hold on my power, knowing it was draining my energy and I'd probably lose hold sooner rather than later anyways. The moment I appeared, the wastelanders seemed to shriek in unison, the shrillness of it making my ears hurt and I watched as the leader of the pack all but shoved one of the male wastelanders in my direction.

As he ran toward me, I used the hurley to pick up a piece of bone and tapped it up in the air, before I smacked it with enough force to make my shoulder scream in pain. The shard lodged in the wastelander's own shoulder, and even though he let out a bellow of pain, he kept coming toward me.

I stood, braced, the hurley in my hands, and waited until he got close enough before I spun out of his advancement, then when he had his back to me, I swung the hurley. The rounded end of the stick hit the base of his skull, the crack echoing throughout the area. Blood and other things hit me in the face as I used my boot to stamp down on his broken skull the moment he hit the ground.

The other wastelanders came at me then with more force, and I let out my own battle cry. The first one that reached me, I slammed the hurley into his stomach, then grabbed a piece of bone from the ground and shoved it into his chest as he doubled over.

The next one that reached me, I rolled out of the way, feeling the sharp sting as I managed to nick myself on the bones, and I smacked the back of its knees to bring it down to my level, before I grabbed another piece of bone and rammed it into its throat.

Fingers grabbed my hair, yanking me up and I elbowed backward. The creature screamed and before I had the chance to react, the fucking thing sank its teeth into my bad shoulder. I screamed, jerking myself forward, and even with my flesh tearing, I swung the hurley. It hit the wastelander in the face, breaking bone, and I screamed again, before unleashing my rage on the thing.

I hit the creature over and over until I was pretty sure there was no face left to hit.

Breathing hard, my gaze darted round to see that I'd taken out most of the wastelanders. The leader of the pack eyed me with curiosity, as if she was trying to figure out that the person that had killed her minions might an asset or something.

I wasn't going to stick around long enough to find out. I took off running, ignoring the way my body wanted to shut down, and climbed up to one of the ledges. Just when I was about to celebrate, a hand grabbed my ankle and dragged me back down.

I guess the leader decided I was better as a meal. Her teeth sank into my leg, and I swung the hurley so hard against her skull, the ash stick splintered, breaking apart.

The wastelander fell to the ground, and I dropped the broken hurley to scramble up and out of the cavern. I made it a few feet before I dropped down, laying on my back as I laughed. I'm sure I was a little delirious as I saw the sign that said welcome to Cork City.

Somehow, I managed to get to my feet, and staggered my way into the city. I must have looked a state, covered in blood and gore, because people kept their distance. I kept going, my head and shoulder pounding, and the bites throbbing, until I found my way to the front gates of my home.

My knees buckled at the realization that I was actually hearing soldiers on the gate shout at me to identify myself. I laughed as the gates opened and the soldiers behind the gate pointed weapons at me. They parted, weapons still aimed, as the leader of the Rebels strode out. If she was surprised to see me, her face certainly didn't show it.

"Hi Mam." I ground out and then everything faded to black.

T he chains bit into my ankles again, causing a flare of heat to burn into my flesh. I didn't try and fight it, because the pain reminded me that I was alive and that there was still a little sliver of hope I could get free. I just needed an opportunity, one moment and I could go home.

I didn't know how long the angels had me held in their prison. The days and nights after a week seemed to bleed into one continuous block of time. The torture and the questioning took most of my focus, trying to make sure the lessons I learned on my path to becoming a soldier had stuck.

So far, I hadn't given the bitch Imperium any solid information, and I could tell that she was getting frustrated. The white-winged bastard was having too much fun breaking my bones and making me scream. I bet he was hoping I'd have the bottle to hold out for a long time, just so he could get himself off on my pain.

There had been a gap in time since they'd last come to

fetch me. The last visitor to my cell was the angel who helped heal all my wounds, his touch even more painful than the sadistic prick who liked to beat me up because, this angel, genuinely believed he was helping me.

I found that out when they had broken four of my ribs and he had healed me. After, I had grabbed his hand and begged him to help me. He just looked at me and told me that he already had, a soft smile on his face. That smile had made me snatch my hand back and I never let myself down by asking for help again.

It had been a few days since they had brought me any food or water, and my stomach rumbled at the mere thought of food. I wasn't even sure there was anyone guarding the other side of my cell right now because I couldn't hear anyone moving about outside.

Probably a blessing in disguise considering the last angel who was guarding my door thought he could take what he wanted from me, but I had kneed him in the balls and bitten him in the face for trying to touch me.

I missed Tiernan. I missed James. Hell, I even missed Hayes and the girls. When I closed my eyes, I could almost hear Tiernan singing. Almost hear James laughing as we sparred. And I could almost smell the bread being baked in the kitchens. I wanted to go home. I just wanted to go home.

It wasn't until I heard myself sob that I realized that I was crying.

My eyes blink open and for a moment, I think my dreams have conjured up home. One quick glance around tells me that I'm in my old room, and nothing had changed since I left for my mission. My heart beats a little faster as the pain in my body seems to catch up with my mind now that it realized that I was awake.

Biting back a whimper of pain, I hear the sound of a page turning and shift my gaze to the right. Tiernan was sat in a chair, his long legs stretched out in front of him, his eyes scanning the book he was reading. He looked like he hadn't slept in days, his eyes tired.

The events that led me here came rushing back and nausea rolled in my stomach. I must have made a sound, because Tiernan became alert, closing his book to look at me, a small smile curving his lips.

"You decided to wake up then, Trouble."

I pulled myself up, and felt my ribs protest as I leaned against the wall, resting my palm on the area just under my breast. "I like keeping you all on your toes. How long was I out?"

"Three days," Tiernan said, then glanced outside. "Almost four. You were in and out all the time. You had an infection you were fighting. And we had to sort your shoulder since it wasn't quite all the way relocated. I'd forgotten how colourful your language could get."

Snorting, I reached over and lifted a glass of water to my lips. "You been sitting there the whole time?"

Tiernan shrugged. "James came and sat with you for a while. You didn't seem to want Hayes here, so it was one of us. Aoife came by too to check on you before she went back to the citadel."

Fuck...the angels had to know I was missing by now.

"Does he know? Does he know I'm here?"

Tiernan shrugged then ran a hand through his hair. "Movement out of the barracks has been restricted. Aoife and maybe a handful of others have been left to leave. It would have looked strange for me to leave you when you were so unwell. That would have made people look at me when we don't need them looking at me."

I set the glass down, my hands trembling. "If he thinks I ran away, then he'll come for me. He won't care if he has to stand facing down an army of Rebels. Nathaniel won't rest until he knows if I escaped."

Tiernan didn't say anything, just sighed. "You live a complicated life, Raven Cassidy."

"Hey, you live that life too buddy."

"Ya, but I don't have an angelic commander lusting after me."

I rolled my eyes, coughed, and that made my ribs flare with pain. "Damn, I never thought I'd actually want to have Adair heal me, but I kinda wish he could right now."

Tiernan got to his feet. "You feel up to a shower? And then I think James would like to see ya. He's been beside himself since you grinned up at your mam, and then passed out right there at the gates. He carried you to the infirmary and held your hand until I could get home."

Swallowing down my emotions, knowing that I had to have been in a bad way when I arrived at the gates, and even though I knew the answer I still asked Tiernan. "Has my mam come to see me at all?"

It was Tiernan's non answering of my question that

told me that Róisín Cassidy hadn't cared enough about her only child to come and see if she had managed to stay alive. Tiernan went over to my chest of drawers and pulled out some clothes, and then grabbed a couple towels. He inclined his head toward the door, and even as I cautiously swung my legs out of the bed, I hesitated.

I didn't need any of the other soldiers seeing me as weak, and I felt like a newborn foal as I placed my feet on the cold floor. I looked at Tiernan, who had packed my things into a backpack, the bag now slung over his shoulder as he held the door open. He must have read my mind because he gave me a warm smile.

"There's no one in this section of the barracks but you and me. Early morning drills are happening in the courtyard. And I think the elders are having a briefing right now in case your fears are founded, and the angels do come in search of you."

I was grateful for the information, and a little worried. My body ached as I tried to walk, and when I stumbled, pitching forward, Tiernan wrapped a strong arm around my waist and led me to the communal showers. Having set the bag with my stuff just outside the shower cubicle, Tiernan leaned against the door to the shower block, his eyes on the floor as I stripped off my clothes and turned on the water.

The spray hit my skin and it hurt, making me wince, but I got down to business and scrubbed my skin, delighted that someone must have washed most of the blood and gore from my skin and hair. I shampooed my hair, running my finger through the tangled length.

When I felt like I was gonna fall down, I turned off the shower and sat on the bench outside with a towel wrapped around me.

"So, you gonna catch me up on what I missed while I was knocked out? Or are you not allowed to tell me anything in case I've been seduced by the angels and the elders need to figure out if I'm friend or foe?"

A muscle ticked in Tiernan's jaw, and I knew I was right.

"It wasn't an order I could refuse, Trouble."

Ah, so mother dearest had ordered Tiernan to keep any vital information from me. I expected that it should have hurt more than it did, but my mother had her reasons and I just had to accept them. I mean, if she had been held captive by the angels for years and then suddenly rocked up at the door, I'd have been sceptical too, right?

I dressed, pulling on knickers and a sports bra, ignoring how the bra made my ribs ache, then pulled on the cargos, and a camo print top. The moment I was dressed in the familiar clothing, it felt like I'd never left, but it also weirdly felt strange, like I was a completely different person to the girl who had once worn these clothes.

Sitting back down on the bench, I pulled on some socks and then my boots, my breathing heavy as I tried to lace them up. Tiernan wordlessly crouched down and lifted my feet so he could lace up my boots. I gave him a smile of thanks as he ruffled my hair as he rose. I snapped the towel out at him, then groaned in pain.

"Did you really fight your way out of the wastelands armed only with a hurley?" Tiernan asked me as I towel dried my hair.

"Ya, it sounds insane when you say it like that, but that's what happened. When did I tell you that?"

"When they were cutting the infection out of the bite on your shoulder. You were ranting and raving, telling us that a sparkly bitch dropped you from the sky and then you beat the wastelanders to death with a hurley."

Shit what else had I said when I was feverish?

Panic made my eyes widen, but Tiernan shook his head. "I distracted you when you started to talk about things that could get you killed. Though everyone is curious to find out what happened between you and Hayes to make you scream at him to get out and even throw a glass at him."

"I don't want you to touch me like that because when you do, I feel absolutely nothing. No, that's a lie. I feel cold, and I hate myself. Nathaniel just has to look at me and I feel goddamn fireworks."

Keeping my gaze averted so Tiernan wouldn't read anything in them, I finished sort of drying my hair, and then gathered it into a ponytail so it was off my face. Tiernan didn't push for an answer, and I was grateful for it. I was glad that I always knew he would have my back, no matter what.

But that made me think of the angels I had come to sort of think of as allies, as friends. Adriel understood the darkness in me more than Tiernan ever would. There is still an optimism in Tiernan that I cling to, like he thinks tomorrow could be better, but Adriel, he doesn't offer fake platitudes. Adriel calls me out on things Tiernan never would.

I hate that I'm comparing them, but they each offer me something I so desperately need to survive. If I was to go to battle with anyone by my side, Tiernan and Adriel would be the first two I would pick. Then I think of Verena and Devika, who spent time with me and have only ever offered me the hand of friendship.

If they all arrived at the gates of the barracks, could I stand by and watch the two parts of me fight against each other?

"You look like you're thinking too hard." Tiernan said softly, like he's afraid to startle me.

I shrugged, my face contorting at the slice of pain in my shoulder. "Is it weak of me to admit that since I've been away for so long, that I'm afraid I won't recognise anyone I know? That things had to have changed since I was gone and what if they never accept me back? And I still have a mission to complete...I don't think the elders will let me get away with not attempting to go back and kill Rieka."

I make to take the bag, but Tiernan gets there before me. We walk back down the hall in silence, with Tiernan not speaking until we had walked back into my room. I sat on the bed, hating how exhausted I felt as Tiernan finally spoke.

"Nothing can stay the same, Raven. I've changed, you've changed. The world around us might stay the same, but it still changes us. The people who love you will accept you. Never be in any doubt of that."

I wanted to say something profound back to him, to tell him that I was still me, but that sounded like a lie. I wasn't sure who I even really was anymore. I had been hiding my true self for so long that I really didn't know who I was when I wasn't lying.

"Why don't you have a rest and then we can go and see James?"

Yawning, I nodded, laying down on the bed as I mumbled. "Just five minutes, that's all I need."

"You lied to me!" It roared; the sound of his indignation almost drowned out by the rumble of thunder.

"I had to." I admitted to it, hoping that somewhere deep inside, the monster might understand why I had to keep my secrets.

Reaching behind its back, the creature withdrew a sword, the metal becoming alight with flames. It was then that I could make out its features, even now, moments before my death, I was struck by how strikingly beautiful the monster from my nightmares was.

His inky black hair glistened with dampness, his storm-filled eyes raging as violently as the storm around us. Sharp cheekbones and a chiselled jaw that I knew felt scratching to touch. His chest was bare, the mark of his rebellion on show for all to see. I had thought that he might understand, that he might sympathize with my plight, with my curse, but the moment he realized that I had lied, I saw my death in his eyes and there was no way to talk myself out of it.

The flames on his sword danced a hungry dance, like they craved the taste of my flesh and were eager to sate that hunger. I looked from right to left, looked for a chance at survival, for a friend to come to my aid and save me from certain death.

But I was alone...there was no one coming to save me... and I could not save myself this time.

"I know what you are."

Frost in his tone, I shifted my gaze back to Nathaniel, and my shoulders slumped. "I know."

Between one breath and the next, Nathaniel stood before me, the heat of his flames almost scorching my skin, but it was the heat of his gaze that threatened to burn me from the inside out. His free hand reached out and gripped my chin with a bruising grasp so I couldn't look away.

"I want to hear you say it. I want to hear it from your own lips. What are you, Raven?"

For a moment, it seemed like the entire world fell away and it was just me and Nathaniel left, not even the weather dared to interfere as I wet my lips and told him. "I'm a Nephilim. I'm half angel."

He growled at me, the fingers on my chin tightening. "A filthy half-breed with deceit in her blood. You fooled us all, Raven. And now I will put an end to your pitiful existence. And if you needed any proof as to why we are monsters, this will surely be enough..."

Nathaniel shoved me away, angling his sword a second before he struck, the blade going into my abdomen, but I felt it in the fragments of my heart. Fire licked at my flesh, the pain searing me as I went down on my knees, my eyes never leaving Nathaniel's as my flesh burnt and he raised the sword, one final slice toward my neck...

I woke with a gasp, struggling to take in air. It was the same damn nightmare that kept haunting me. I couldn't make myself take a breath and it was the feel of Tiernan resting a hand on my back, rubbing comforting circles as he told me to breathe in through my nose and out my mouth.

"It's okay, Raven. I got you."

When my breathing finally went back to normal, I leaned my head back against Tiernan. "Sorry."

"That happen a lot?"

"I'm afraid if I say yes then you'll never let me out of your sight again."

I got up off the bed and faced Tiernan's frowning face. Turning away, I fixed my hair and then nodded to the door. "Can we go see James now?"

Tiernan looked like he wanted to ask me more about my nightmares, yet he still got up and we headed down toward the main courtyard. My appearance by Tiernan's side earned me a few curious glances as we started to encounter people, but I ignored them. Tiernan kept glancing at me with a worried expression, then he held open the door to the courtyard, and then stepped up beside me.

Memories of us all training, sparring, and messing about came rushing back as I watched a hell of a lot more Rebels training then when I left to go to the citadel. Our numbers had grown, but the recruits seemed younger, which sat uneasy with me as I remembered Noelle and the way her neck snapped in my hands.

"There's more than I was expecting."

"And more come every day. We had someone from the north arrive last week and he said there were hundreds of humans in the Seraphan held location that want to fight alongside us."

That was both thrilling and terrifying all at once.

THREE

"Y ou want me to call him, or do you want to do the honours?"

My eyes dart to where a familiar man is sparring shirtless with another soldier, his dark hair sleek with sweat and sharp green eyes scanning his opponent for their next move. Much like Tiernan, he had a beard and a scruff to him that had grown now that he was no longer a teen. The jagged scar that ran down from his left eye, one that I now knew Makata was responsible for, was ever present.

The soldier lunged for James, then after dodging the strike, James got cocky, and goaded the soldier with a kick in the ass as he stumbled past James. That meant that James had his back to me.

A slow smirk curved my lips. "Oh, let me."

Putting my fingers in my mouth, I whistled, long and loud and then sounded. "Sloppy, Barnes! Call yourself a goddamn soldier? I've seen toddlers with more grace than you!"

James' head snapped round, and his eyes widened even as his mouth opened, and the soldier took that as his chance. He kicked the back of James' knees, and my friend went down to the ground, but the psychotic bastard was grinning as he jumped to his feet and started toward me.

We met in the middle and James hugged me too him. I ignored the pain in my ribs, and the way my shoulder protested. The warmth in my chest was worth the pain. I heard James mumble against my hair, then felt wetness, and knew the soft git was crying.

When we stepped apart, his eyes were red, but his smile was so bright, it nearly blinded me.

"Alright, Superhero, dry your eyes or people will start to talk about us!

James chuckled at the nickname, given to him when we found out his Ma had named him after her favourite comic book character, brushing his knuckles against my jaw. "They already talk about me, Raven. Just helps spread my infamy."

I snorted. "Still a cocky little shit I see."

"Still determined to dance with death, I see."

Rolling my eyes, I let him pull me back in for a hug, until Tieran tapped him on the shoulder. "Jay, don't push it. She's still healing."

That made James jerk back out of our embrace. "Shit, did I hurt you?"

Shaking my head, I gave James a big grin. "Nah, I've

being spending my time getting smacked about by angel's wings, a little hug isn't gonna kill me."

James' gaze narrowed. "What the fuck is that supposed to mean?"

Sighing, I motioned for James to follow me, so we could move away from all the curious ears around us. I went over to the wall, then slid down so I could stretch out my legs. James came to sit to my right, and Tiernan sat by my left and it almost, almost felt like old times.

"Listen, it's not a big deal. I was ordered to find an angel in the citadel under the promise I'd be let go, and he was able to hurt me by smacking his wing into me. It made me loose control of my power and so I asked the angel I was training with to hit me with his wings to desensitize myself to the pain. That's it."

"Did it work?" James asked me, and I laughed.

"Still hurts like a bitch but it's easier to take once you feel it over a dozen times or so."

James scratched his beard. "Huh, that actually sounds smart...are you sure it was your idea?"

Laughing again, I shoved at his shoulder. "Asshole."

We lapsed into a comfortable silence, one of familiarity, reminding me of the many days and nights we had sat beside each other on duty, sometimes never needing to say a word. When I left that day to go and kill Rieka, I never imagined we would all be sitting here together again.

"I've missed you guys." I mumbled softly, as James yanked a strand of my hair.

"We missed you too. It was hell, thinking they had

killed you but when we found out you were alive, fuck, Raven, we wanted to advance on the citadel and bring you home. Though none of us expected you to be the one to bring yourself home."

I chuckled, leaning my head against the wall, closing my eyes. "On the bad days, and there were a lot, after the torture and shit, I'd close my eyes in my cell and remember happy memories. Tiernan singing around the fire with his guitar. James swindling everyone out of their valuables by pretending he didn't count cards. The laughter. The friendship. The hope of seeing you guys again kept me alive."

Tieran twined his fingers into mine, gave my hand a squeeze.

"They tortured you."

It was a statement rather than a question, but I had to answer James anyways or else he would start to conjure scenarios in his head and that was worse than knowing the truth. Our James might be the first person to offer a joke or a smile, but he worried as much, if not more than Tiernan.

"Ya, they skipped over the part where they tried to gain my trust and offer me nice things to start talking. The Imperium, she was all for inflicting pain on me since I almost succeeded in killing her. They had a healer who would heal all my broken bones and bring me back to life when my heart gave out. It was like rinse and repeat for days, then they left me alone in the dark for days, maybe weeks, and then it started again."

James cursed, shaking his head and his leg started to

bounce. I reached over and let my hand rest on his knee. "It's okay. We knew it might happen. The elders wondering if seeing a young girl would make them think twice about retribution, but it didn't. I'd still be rotting in the prison if it wasn't for the commander asking me to search for their rogue angel."

"And you and the commander? Are the rumours that he has a thing for you true?"

My heart did a little double tap in my chest. How did I explain it to my best friends without betraying my secret? How could I explain to them that whatever was between me and Nathaniel, it was a connection that neither of us could explain. Like a moth to a flame, we couldn't stay away from one another, and it would be the death of us both.

Instead of being honest, knowing that Tieran was fully aware of the bubbling tension between me and Nathaniel, and James seemed to be oblivious to Tieran and Nathaniel's allegiance, I just shrugged my shoulders and grinned. "Of course he has. I'm a fucking delight, how could he resist."

James barked out a laugh, the sound carrying across the courtyard as the gates opened and Hayes strode in pulling a trailer behind him. My mood immediately darkened when our eyes clashed, and I felt a small petty victory when he looked away first.

"You need to keep him away from the citadel." I told both the men sitting beside me. "He's going to give himself away and get himself killed."

"He's always been in love with you, Trouble. He's jealous of the attention the commander is giving you."

"And it will get him killed. You have sway, Tiernan. If you tell the elders he has compromised himself or whatever diplomatic shit you have to sprout, they will stop him going to the citadel and that will keep him alive. If I have to go back, then keep him away."

Tiernan squeezed my hand. "I will do my best. I promise."

Hayes put the brake on the trailer, then grabbed something from the back and came toward us. I braced myself for him to make a snide comment, to just come out and throw shade at me but he just dropped to the ground, reached into the bag he had and tossed a bag at each of us.

I arched a brow, then opened the bag, almost groaning when I spotted the boiled sweets. Hayes snorted, shaking his head and when I glared at him, he shrugged. "Anytime you were mad at any of us, we knew we could win you round with food. I made sure to stop off on my way back at that shop that makes sweets."

I frowned as James and Tieran laughed, though I still popped one of the sweets into my mouth, the taste of crisp apple making me make little sounds that had the others cracking up. Was I that easy to bribe?

"I haven't forgiven you yet."

"I'll take the sweets back then." Hayes said, his tone light and teasing.

"You will fucking not." I replied as I tossed another sweet into my mouth. "I might be injured but I can still knock you on your ass with one arm tied behind my back."

For a moment Hayes looked like he might try and take my sweets from me, then he leaned back on his arms and stretched out his legs. Even though I was still pissed off at him, this was the most relaxed I'd felt in a long time. Back at the citadel, I was always on the edge, waiting for something to happen, or an attack to come. I was always afraid that my secret would come out and even though the guys didn't know what I was, I held onto the hope that they wouldn't care.

"What news from the citadel, Hayes?"

The sound of Tiernan's voice dragged me from my thoughts. I ate another sweet and then stored the rest away in the pocket of my cargos for later. I shifted to lean against James' shoulder, closing my eyes so I couldn't see Hayes looking at me like he was.

"The League of Dominious have closed ranks. Rumours are circling around the citadel that Raven has escaped. Molly is trying to push that over the rumour that Raven has been killed by the Imperium. The commander has claimed that Raven is unwell, struck down with a virus and stopped the steady flow of visitors to her room."

I swallowed hard, imagining what chaos my disappearance would be causing at the citadel.

"Do they know that it was Saskia?" I asked quietly.

"I'm not sure. She hasn't been seen in since the night you vanished. The commander hasn't slept in days. He wears that axe he gave you on a belt on his waist."

I didn't know if that was a comfort or not.

"Molly said one of the girls overheard the healer and your attendant talking. She wanted to see you, but the healer said that they just had to let you rest and he was doing all he could to help you get better. They all seem very worried for you."

There was a note of something in Hayes' tone that had me opening my eyes and glaring right at him. "If you have something to say, then just say it."

His face dropped, and he looked away, but all the bullshit production of bringing back sweets and trying to play nice was suddenly washed away with that one sly remark. Hayes opened his mouth to retort, then shook his head like he thought better of it.

"Oh don't be shy now, Hayes. I'm surprised you are not talking more shite about me playing nice with the angels. You've done nothing since you found out that I was alive but look down your nose at me for how I chose to survive. You scoff at the fact that I might call an angel my friend, when some of them have treated me better than you have."

Hayes looked venomous as his face contorted. "Do the men you call brothers know that you've been kissing angels? Or that you don't look like a fucking prisoner when you are swanning about the halls laughing and joking with members of the League like they are your besties?"

His voice has risen, and then he does, like he's ready to storm off like a petulant child. I surged to my feet, anger a steady boil in my veins. I feel it the moment Tiernan and James get to their feet and have my back.

"Don't you fucking dare. Don't you dare presume to know what it's been like for me. Were you the one who had every finger broken in her hands only for them to heal them to start the process over again? Were you the one who had to fight off angels who thought to try and *rape* you while I fucking chained to a wall?"

Hayes had the decency to look horrified at my proclamation, and I can't ignore the sudden intakes of breath from the men standing at my side. My hands were trembling, but I'm not done yet.

"Were you the one who had to play like she was the Imperium's private sniffer fucking dog, constantly on guard because I know I can't trust anyone? I've been beaten. I've been electrocuted. I've been burned. I've been dropped from the fucking sky and had to relocate my shoulder so I could fight my way out of the wastelands with a goddamn hurley to come home to my family."

I stepped right up to Hayes and we were almost the same height. He looks shocked by my revelations, like he really expected that I'd been having a right good time since I went to the citadel. I jabbed a finger into his chest, looking him dead in the eye. "You wouldn't hold up to that level of interrogation. You never could. You couldn't survive half of what was done to me so you don't get to judge me for thinking maybe one or two angels were half decent. Considering you turned out to be such an asshole."

I shoved Hayes away from me with a growl, knowing if he opened his mouth to say any more, I'd be ready for a physical fight and I would give him a taste of what it was like to be beaten within an inch of your life. He's just standing there, looking at me like he's not believing I just told him all of what I did.

"Ya, it happened. If you don't want the truth, don't ask me or throw around petty comments. If you want things to be sugar-coated, go eat a fucking donut or something. Now get out of my face before I hurt you."

Hayes looked like he was about to argue with me, but Tiernan stepped forward, reaching out to grasp Hayes on the shoulder. "Let it be for today, Hayes. Give her some space."

He jerked away from Tiernan, and stormed off toward the barracks and I blew out a breath, exhaustion weighing me down. James bounced forward, a stupid grin on his face. "I thought you were going to kill him."

"I can't say I wasn't tempted." I told him, then watched as his smile fell.

"Did an angel really try and assault you?"

I gave a very dispassionate shrug of my shoulders. "Um ya, not just one. It stopped when I managed to wrap the chains around a certain appendage and twist until it snapped. I made it clear that I wasn't the kind of girl to give them what they wanted without a fight."

James was still for a moment, then he mock punched me in the jaw with his fist. "That's our girl. Now, do I have to go all big brother on your sassy ass and ask what the hell Hayes meant when he said you were kissing angels?"

I rolled my eyes. This was definitely not a conversation I was having with James, even if the idiot had only said it to draw us away from the pretty terrible things I'd revealed in my outburst.

"How bout we stop grilling Raven and go and get something solid to eat? Hayes might be a bit of a dick, but he wasn't wrong when he said the way to Raven's affections was her stomach."

This time, I shoved Tiernan and he laughed, before slinging an arm around my shoulders. We head to the mess hall, where Tiernan led me to a table in the furthest corner, away from the curious stares and the whispers. James went to fetch us some food, his expression daring anyone to even have a go at me.

When he came down with the stew, the moment the scent hit my nose, I went fully feral and began shovelling large spoonfuls into my mouth. Tiernan mumbled at me to slow down or I'd end up with indigestion, shoving his bowl toward me when I devoured mine, before getting up to get another bowl for himself.

"Damn, Raven, did they not feed you in the citadel?"

Shaking my head, I did the very ladylike thing of answering with my mouth full. "No one cooks stew like the Irish. And they fed me, but it's hard to enjoy food when you always have to assume it might be poisoned."

Tiernan came back then with another bowl, and a slice of cake that had me pushing aside my empty bowl and dragging the plate across the table. Using a fork, I took a piece of the cake and moaned when I put the thing in my mouth, the burst of flavour like actual divinity.

"Lieutenant Cassidy."

It took me a moment to realize that someone was talking to me. No one had called me by my rank in so long, it sounded foreign to hear someone saying it now. I glanced to my right, saw a young recruit standing a little away from the table.

"Yes, recruit?"

He swallowed hard, a bead of sweat on his brow as the boys turned to look at him too. He looked almost starstruck, like he couldn't find the words to speak.

"Spit, it out recruit." Tiernan said gently but firmly.

"Yes, Captain. Um...the elders have requested your presence, Lieutenant Cassidy. They await you in the briefing room."

Ah, so my interrogation was gonna start.

Hey, I was just glad they let me eat first. Small mercies and all that crap...

CHAPTER

FOUR

I take my time and finish my cake, the recruit squirming and sweating like a pig on a stick because I hadn't jumped up and followed him like he expected me to. When I finished the last crumb of the cake, I picked up the plate and licked it clean. Tiernan and James were laughing so hard the two idiots were almost crying.

"Lieutenant Cassidy, the elders seemed eager to speak to you."

"I'm sure they are." I retorted with a snort. "But considering I've been a prisoner of war and almost died several times, I'm gonna sit here a few minutes more and enjoy my cake before I go and see the elders."

I knew that everyone was watching the interaction. I needed to assert my rank and the power I hoped I still held. With a slow, almost feral smile, I locked eyes with the recruit, watched as he swallowed hard as I said. "If

39

you have a problem with that, recruit, you can sure as hell try and drag me there."

Pulling my power to me, I heard a few screams, and then I reappeared behind the recruit and whispered boo in his ear. He let out a yelp, and then his eyes widened, and he almost pissed himself. James and Tiernan were still laughing, but they got to their feet as if to come with me, but the scaredy little recruit looked almost panicked.

"Captain Byrne, Lieutenant Barnes, the elders only requested to speak to Lieutenant Cassidy."

The smile faded from Tiernan's face and James went rigid by his side. Me? I was trying very hard not to laugh.

"Are you trying to give me an order, recruit?" Tiernan's tone was ice cold and menacing.

"No, uh, sir. I was just repeatin' what the elders told me."

Tiernan folded his arms across his chest. "Lieutenant Cassidy is a member of my squad. I am well within my rights to accompany her to any debriefing about her captivity and had you read your rule book more thoroughly, then you would have known that and not wasted our time with inconsequential statements."

I was fairly certain that this time, the recruit was about to piss himself for real.

"Dismissed, recruit. I'm sure we can find the briefing room by ourselves."

The recruit glanced over his shoulder at me, and I just shrugged. Then he took off like his pants were on fire and the mess hall was still silent. Turning round to face them, I grinned, waving my hand in the air. "Show's over folks. Eat your dinner before it gets cold. We can't be wasting food."

We walked out of the mess hall, then the three of us burst out laughing. Tears rolled down our faces as I braced a hand on the wall, my ribs not at all happy that I was willingly doing something that made them no so happy. I tried to stop, because I really was going to face an interrogation.

"Lads, stop laughing. My ribs are fucking killing me."

James wiped tears from his eyes. "Damn, that was fun. We haven't that much fun taking the piss out of the newbies since you left."

When we had composed ourselves and were not acting like teenagers, we headed down the hall. The boys flanked me as we made our way to the briefing room, and I tried to steel myself against what might happen once I went through the door. Tiernan had spoken true when he said as my captain, he could come in with me, but how did I tell him I was afraid that the elders might use both him and our friendship against me?

"I can see the wheels turning in your mind, Trouble. I've got your six in there."

Two soldiers stood sentry at the doors to the briefing room, and when they made to open the doors, Tiernan held up his hand. He faced me, rested his hands on my shoulders, his face stern. "Do not give them something to hold against you. Do not talk back or offer any sarcastic retort. Just give them what they want and then we will walk out of that room, and everything will be alright. You hear me?"

"Loud and clear."

Tiernan leaned in and kissed my forehead. "Good girl."

James nodded in my direction, then went to the wall opposite the door, leaned against it, and folded his arms across his chest to wait until my debrief was done. I pivoted, facing the door, felt Tiernan fall in beside me and then he nodded, and the doors opened.

Together, we strode into the room, stopping at a reasonable distance from the table where four people sat, including my mother. We came to attention and saluted. I wasn't sure if it was a play of power, or what, but they left us there for a while before lifting their heads to even acknowledge our presence. I had to remind myself of what Tiernan said because I'd gotten used to talking back to those who claimed to have the authority to order us about.

My mother sat second from the left of the row, the leadership seat. She was dressed in a similar fashion to what I was wearing, her black hair pulled back into a stern looking bun that showed off the angles of her face. Blue eyes, darker than mine by a shade or two, watched me, but her expression didn't give anything away.

Beside my mother to her left sat Seamus Kennedy, Hayes' father. He looked like an older version of Hayes, but with a more rounded belly that came from giving orders instead of taking them. He ran his eyes over me, assessing me, and sneered.

Ah so his son was reporting back to daddy about me...

Next to Seamus was Caoimhe Clarke, Niamh's

mother. She gave me the only warm smile I was gonna get from the four sitting behind the table. Niamh's mother wasn't a soldier, but she had been a garda, a police officer, before the world went to shit and she was the head of the spy network that her daughter effectively ran with her.

Must be nice to work with your child instead of sending her off to get killed, right?

To my mother's left, I expected to see Donnacha Lynch but in his place was his son Eoghan, Aoife's step-brother. He was a couple of years older than Tiernan, too young to be considered an elder but there he was, right beside the leader of the Rebels...but what had happened to Donnacha.

"At ease soldiers."

The first words my mother had spoken to me since I arrived back, and it was an order. We relaxed our stance, clasping our hands behind our backs, and waited. The elders made a point of looking through some papers. Caoimhe looked at my mother, shook her head, then lifted her gaze to me.

"It is good to see that you are recovered from your ordeal, Raven."

My mother's gaze slid to Caoimhe, then back to her papers.

I really wasn't sure which of my many ordeals Caoimhe was referring to, so I just replied. "Thank you, Ma'am."

"Have you rested enough? I am certain this could be done at later date."

"I'm fine, Ma'am. I appreciate the concern."

Caoimhe sighed, shaking her head, then Aoife's step-brother looked at Tiernan standing by my side. "Captain, you can take your leave. We can speak with Lieutenant Cassidy alone."

Tiernan stiffened beside me, and I wanted to turn to him and tell him to go, but he looked at Eoghan, then replied. "I would stay. The lieutenant is one of mine, has been since the day your father gave her to me to prepare for war. If it was any other member of my squad, I'd still be standing here. If you order me to leave, then I will do so. But I would stay."

"The girl is yours now. Train her, prepare her. Take her on missions with you."

I think that was the moment when I'd officially become Tiernan's, his family, but our bond was forged well before that. Blood I'd learned was nothing when it came to family. We shared no blood in common, only the blood spilled in war, and Tiernan had more love for me then the woman who gave birth to me.

"As you wish. You can stand back though. I'm sure the Lieutenant doesn't need you to hold her hand."

Asshole...

Tiernan did as he was told, though I knew he wanted to stand beside me. I lifted my head, almost defiantly and waited them out. If they thought the delay tactic would get on my nerves, they were right, and yet, I had spent a long time in the angel's prison. I could wait them out.

"Lieutenant Cassidy." My mother finally spoke to me,

her tone was monotone, as if she were already bored of this conversation.

"Lieutenant-general." I said in response, earning me a nod of acknowledgement.

"Just to assuage Colonel Clarke's motherly instinct, you are well enough to answer some questions we have for you?"

"Yes, Lieutenant-general."

"Good." My mother said, then looked at Eoghan. "You can begin, Brigadier general."

Well, that was an interesting nugget of information. Eoghan Lynch outranked Caoimhe Clarke by a single rank. His father had been the last Brigadier general. Looks like his title had been inherited rather than earned like the rest of us.

Eoghan nodded his head at my mother. "Lieutenant Cassidy, can you explain what happened on the night you were to kill the Imperium?"

Christ, that seemed like such a long time ago, far longer than the, what, four years it had been? I closed my eyes for a moment, trying to remember all the little details. "I failed. That's what happened. I had been working the floor as part of the human waitstaff, and had waited until the angels were nice and relaxed. Private Kennedy handed me the dagger and I used my power to go invisible. I stood beside the Imperium, and I struck."

That was the night Nathaniel had come crashing into my life and set my path off track. "The Commander of the League of Dominious could see through my power and he tackled me as I went to stab the Imperium. The blade ended up in her shoulder instead of her chest. I was dragged and imprisoned then for three years."

"Have you ever been able to ascertain how the Commander could see through your power?"

I shook my head. "No, sir. I've never been able to figure it out."

Eoghan frowned, inclining his head, and then it was Hayes' father who spoke next. "Can you outline some of the things that happened to you during your three years of captivity?"

He said it so coldly, like no matter what I said, he really didn't fucking care because at the end of it all, I'd failed in my mission. I'd failed in not dying for my country and taking out the Angel's leader. That was my biggest sin.

"Of course, sir. I was chained to a wall in the darkest part of the dungeons. They chained me up after I attacked my guards and tried to take my own life by jumping out the window to a cavern below. During my time in captivity, I was subjected to interrogation quite a lot. Sometimes daily. Isolation, sleep deprivation, they sometimes forgot to feed me or give me water for weeks. Torture, broken bones, multiple attempted sexual assaults." That had my mother looking at me, but I continued. "I was left to face the elements, sometimes rain flooding the room. I caught a sickness and was left to fend off the fever without aid."

"When you say multiple attempted sexual assault, Raven?" Caoimhe asked me gently. "Can you elaborate?"

I swallowed to put some moisture in my suddenly dry mouth. "Of course, Ma'am. I had been captive just a few days when one of the angels started looking at me in a sexual way. I stabbed him with a piece of branch that had come in with the wind. Time evaded me after a few weeks, but the second angel waited until I was chained before he put his hands on me."

"But no assault took place?" Seamus asked.

"No. I broke his cock with my chains and told them that anyone else who dared to come and have a go at me, I'd bite off their appendages, sir."

I heard a chuckle over my shoulder, and I wanted to laugh, but I couldn't. "There was one more, quite recently. Though many would say I brought it on myself. I goaded the angel, made him look like a fool, and then we fought. If it had not been for the Commander and one of his League, Adriel, then I'm certain Abraxas would have raped me."

"Keep struggling. I like it."

Closing my eyes, I felt a wave of panic well inside my chest. I tried to reign it in, knowing it was not a good idea to break down in front of the people who would determine if I was too damaged to go back in the field or not.

"Shit, fuck, I mean." I stopped talking, pushed everything down and then opened my eyes to see everyone staring at me. "My apologies, sirs, Ma'am. The attack is unfortunately still quite fresh."

"Might I ask what the Commander did to the angel, since it seems he so venomously defended your honour?"

47

"He ripped off his wings and burned them. They will grow back, but it will take a while. And it's painful."

"So, the rumours of the Commander's...affection...for you are true."

My mother's question wasn't unexpected. This was where I needed to lie. If they knew the full extent of what Nathaniel thought he felt for me, then she would order him dead and that would truly start a new kind of war. Rieka would lose her shit, and she would come for us all.

"We had an understanding. I was useful to him due to my power, and our agreement meant that I was able to regain my strength and train and try and gather information. Though that has been harder with the commander being able to see me even when invisible."

"And the fact that you have been making friends with the angels is something we are meant to brush aside?" Eoghan asked, a lick of venom in his tone.

"Keep your friends close, sir, and your enemies even more so. The angels have spent a considerable amount of time trying to persuade me that they are not all monsters, and letting them think that they are swaying me, that gave me more freedom in the citadel."

My mother leaned back in her chair. "What do you think of the angels now, Lieutenant Cassidy? Have they managed to sway you like they hoped?"

I should lie, I should tell my mother that they are all monsters and I wanted them all dead, but she would know if I lied. She'd always been able to know. It was one of our rules. We didn't lie to one another. My mother had a lot of rules for me to follow. She expected me to follow orders. To never back down. To show respect to those in charge. To bleed for the cause. To show no mercy. To be the perfect soldier, and to always have a plan to kill everyone in the room.

"I think that the world is fucked. There are monsters on both sides. But just like humans have the capacity for good, then so can an angel. But if you want to question my loyalty to the cause, then let me assure you that should a choice come between saving a human life and killing an angel who showed me compassion, then the tools I have gained at the citadel will aid me to strike down any angel, one considered friend or foe, so no human blood needs to be shed."

My mother tilted her head to the side, a slight smirk on her face and I wonder if I have pleased her or disappointed her with my answer. "If I asked you to outline the strengths and weaknesses of the Imperium's elite soldiers, you would tell us without hesitation."

"Yes Ma'am."

"And," Eoghan began and I dragged my gaze to his as he said. "If we asked you to return to the citadel, to finish your botched mission, what would you say?"

"How soon do you want me to leave, sir? Had you not asked it of me, I would have suggested it. My mission is not yet complete, and I would love to have Rieka's blood on my fucking hands."

"Be that as it may," Seamus interjects, resting his elbows on the table. "And despite your very convincing argument of why you have been seen cozying up to the angels, the fact remains that after almost four years away, it is a reasonable thinking that you may have been tainted to the angel's way of thinking."

Anger punched through me. "With all due respect, Sir, I wasn't off having shits and giggles with the angels. I was *tortured*. I was beaten to a pulp, healed, and then rinse and repeat until it almost killed me. I did what I did to stay alive and no one in this room, hell, even in this fucking barracks has bled more for her country than me. You don't believe me? Fine. Let me show you."

Without waiting, I stripped off my t-shirt, showing the scarring to my front and then I did a slow rotation, making sure everyone got a good look at the marks on my skin. I pulled back on my t-shirt and showed my hands, calloused, and scarred to.

And then I forgot what Tiernan had told me and looked a pale Seamus dead in the eyes. "My body is marked for every time I bled for the cause. My hands are calloused and weathered from fighting for our race. Tell me, Major-general, how calloused are your hands from all the paper pushing you fucking do?"

Seamus's face turned a violent shade of red as my mother gave me a stern look. "That is enough, Lieutenant."

"My apologies, Ma'am. Perhaps Colonel Clarke was correct, and I am still recovering from my ordeal. Pardon my outburst."

Caoimhe was holding back a smile as she ducked her head and Seamus looked like he wanted to kill me. He'd have to get in line though, there was already a fuckton of people who wanted me dead.

I can tell that Eoghan wants to grill me some more. His eyes are eager, too eager and I know he is trying to impress my mother. Poor fucker. I wanted to tell him that he'd never be able to live up to the impossible standards that Róisín Cassidy set for those around her. I knew from experience, of course, having spent my entire childhood trying to impress her, to make her proud.

Then I see it, the way Eoghan looks at my mother.

Well...that's unexpected...they're having sex.

My mother looked at me and I arched a brow, though nothing in her face gave anything away. Eoghan opened his mouth to speak, but there comes an urgent knocking on the door and then a recruit bursts in and she is gasping for air.

Tiernan looked at me and I nodded, and he bolts from the room. I'm itching to follow him, because I know that something is amiss, however, if I walk out that door without being dismissed, it might undo anything I've done to convince them that I am not a traitor.

"Spit it out, recruit." My mother demanded, and the recruit trembled at the sound of her voice.

I walked over to the young girl, put a hand on her chest to help her focus on breathing. When she has caught her breath, I asked her what was going on, and then her next words almost gave me a heart attack.

"Angels. They're here. In the courtyard. They've come looking for the Lieutenant."

I glanced over my shoulder and my mother gives one swift incline of her head and I take off. My boots thunder down the hallway as I try and duck and weave through the chaos. Everyone is trying to get to the courtyard to defend the barracks while I'm just wanting to get outside to prevent a blood bath on both sides.

Everyone is scrambling to get weapons, the fear among them is so palpable I can almost smell it. When I get to the doors leading to the courtyard, I can't get through the crowd of people. Some look like they've seen their deaths, others look entranced by their first sighting of an angel up close. My stomach does somersaults as I wonder who Rieka has sent to fetch me, or if this is someone coming to tell my mother I'm dead...

I mean, it would totally be hilarious to see their faces if they actual think I'm dead.

Shoving my way through the crowd, I'm thinking I might have to physically hurt some of my fellow soldiers to get them to move. I can see a battalion poised at the gates, ready to fire. In front of them, I can see Tiernan, his red hair like a beacon in the dimly lit courtyard. James stood at the opposite side, a crossbow in his hands, aimed and ready to fire at a magenta haired angel.

Fuck, James was face-to-face with the angel who had disfigured him and the idiot was grinning like a damn idiot. Tiernan had a shotgun aimed at an angel I couldn't see, his face grim and his shoulders tense, but I almost skidded to a halt when I finally was able to get a clear sight of what everyone was looking at.

Hayes was front and centre of the soldiers blocking the gates, a trio of other soldiers standing next to him. Looked like Hayes had found some dumbasses to follow his lead. They all looked extremely trigger happy, angelic blood being spilled high on their agenda, but as I forced my way around and through the battalion, I stopped dead when I saw who Hayes was glaring at.

Hayes had a bolt gun aimed at Nathaniel and I knew that he was itching to fire it. It was written all over his stupid face. I could see Hayes' little sheep waiting for him to give the order and I had to stop this from turning into a bloodbath that brought the war right to our fucking door.

I had to show all the fucking minions who truly had the most power around here and I might have been gone for four years, but when you walk or well collapsed at the gates after everyone assumed you were dead, myth and legend could be a powerful thing indeed.

I stepped into view, ignoring the heat in Nathaniel's gaze when he spotted me striding forward. I gave the angels my back, showing the entire barracks of humans that I was not afraid, and I focused on Hayes.

Tiernan had a gun aimed at Adriel, but I knew he'd never take the shot unless provoked. Hayes would do it and claim that his finger slipped.

"Stand down, Private." I ordered Hayes as I stepped in his direct line of sight and took Nathaniel out of his firing line. The bolt gun pressed into the spot where my heart was beating, and now, that slip of a finger would kill me, not Nathaniel.

Hayes' jaw clenched as I arched a brow, but he refused to follow my order.

"Stand the fuck down, Private." I growled, lifting my hand to rest on the bolt gun. "In case you forgot, *Private*, I fucking outrank you unless you've been promoted in the four years I've been gone? No? Well, if you don't want me to kick your ass and make you bleed in front of your fan club you will do as fucking ordered, soldier and stand the fuck down. Don't make me tell you a fucking third time."

The threat was implied. I would lay him out on the cold hard ground if he didn't follow the order. There was a heartbeat where I thought Hayes wouldn't back down but then he slowly lowered his gun as I heard a dark chuckle from behind me, which I ignored.

"Good boy." I said, adding salt in his wounds, making his jaw clench, and he looked at me like he hated me. I could live with that. "Go and make yourself useful and get the fuck away from me."

"Fine." He ground out and turned to leave, but I put a booted foot on top of his, forcing him to look back at me.

"You wanna try that again?" I told him with a cold-ness in my tone that had him obey.

"Yes, Lieutenant."

I held his gaze for a moment or two more, then inclined my head sharply allowing Hayes and his little kiss asses to disappear into the crowd. Rolling my shoulders, I turned to face the angels. They were dressed for battle, though no weapons graced their hands, because they were the weapon.

Nathaniel stood watching me with an avid curiosity. Adriel had a slight smile curving his lips, like he was proud of the display that I had just put on. Makata only had eyes for James. Devika waved at me from behind Nathaniel, and I lifted my hand in greeting, though kept my expression bland.

For the longest time, no one said anything. I rolled my eyes and skipped my gaze over to look at Adriel, who still looked slightly amused. In the end, it was my friend who spoke first as I fought the urge to go to him.

"Just a soldier, Lieutenant?"

I shrugged. "I was never one for fancy titles and shit. But if I get to pull rank on stupid pricks, then I'll use it when I need to."

Adriel chuckled, shaking his head. "You were late to training."

"This time it really wasn't my fault. It's not every day Sparkles tries to kill you by dropping you into the wastelands."

His eyes assess me, as if looking for an injury. His black and green wings flared, and I knew that he was worried about me. "I'm grand. I wasn't gonna let Saskia be the one to kill me."

"Good girl." His tone was full of praise, and it reminded me that it was more than I would ever get from my own mother. My stomach clenched, knowing I was keeping a massive secret from Adriel that could sever any relationship that we had, and that would kill me.

"Right then. So ye found out Saskia threw a fit and decided the best course of action was to rock up to Rebel HQ for a not so friendly chat?"

Adriel gave me a deadpanned expression. "I think I've spent too much time around you, Raven. I decided to flirt with death a little bit more than usual. You are a bad influence."

My mouth hung open at his jibe, and then I heard Tiernan laughing beside me. I turned to glare at him, and he shrugged, before saying. "Hey, he's not wrong. That's kinda funny."

Sighing, I rubbed my temple, then looked at James. He still hadn't taken his eyes off Makata, his hostility almost as palpable as the way Hayes' hatred of Nathaniel had been. But I didn't think he hated her as much as I was suspecting.

"You don't remember me, do ya, gorgeous?" James said, giving Makata his best flirtatious smile.

"Should I?" she ground out, her wings twitching like she was uncomfortable at the scrutiny.

"Ah, darling, you're bruising me ego here."

"I'm sure you'll recover." Makata drawled, and she blinked, like she had surprised herself. I wanted to tell

James to cool it, that Makata had lost her mate, raised her son by herself and didn't need him flirting with her.

"Last time we met, darling, you gave me a nice little souvenir." He pointed to the scar on his face. "I haven't stopping thinking bout ya since that day."

Makata blinked, her magenta eyes widening. "That was you?" James winked and Makata's cheeks went pink. "I thought you meant to harm the boy. It was only after that my son told me you tried to shield him."

Realization dawned in James and his expression softened. "Ah shite, I didn't know he was your son. Understandable that you'd defend him. You could make it up to me with a kiss, though darling. You did ruin my beautiful face."

"James, stop flirting and act like a solider, ya fecking idiot!" I shouted at him, which to be fair, only makes him grin even more as he blew a kiss at Makata, who looked away and at anything but the man flirting with her.

A throat cleared. I lifted my gaze to look at Nathaniel. His eyes were filled with storms I couldn't decipher, this pull, this magnetism between us had me taking a step closer at the exact moment that he did. His broad shoulders and torso were covered in his armour, but I knew there were coiled muscles underneath his clothing.

My skin heated and my heart started to gallop and that made Nathaniel smile at me with a smugness that reminded me of our conversation before I found out that Nathaniel and Tiernan had an alliance.

"You can hear my heartbeat? Can you hear it all the time?"

A slight smirk tugged at the corners of his mouth. "Not consciously. Angelic hearing is better than a human's, as are all our other senses. But as everything is louder, I have to focus to be able to drown out other sounds. In this quiet, yes, I can hear your heartbeat."

The damn organ started to pick up pace then as Nathaniel's smile deepened. "Does that worry you, Raven?"

I realized that I've been too lost in the memory when I feel the heat of Nathaniel's palm on my cheek as he speaks the first words to me. "I'm glad to see that you are okay."

Behind me, I could hear the shocked collective gasp, a chorus of outrage ensues among them, and I know that I have to try and protect Nathaniel and everyone I care about, even if it means hurting him a little to do so.

I retreated, taking a step back and his hand falls. "I'm fine, commander. I wasn't about to let your ex kick my ass. I hope she's suffering for trying to have me eaten alive by wastelanders."

"Saskia is spending some quality time with Verena."

A slow smirk curved my lips. I hoped that V was delving as fucking deep into Saskia's airhead brain as possible and pulling on her worst fears. I hoped the dumb bitch screamed and screamed until her throat was torn and then they had Adair heal her so that Verena could do it all over again.

"What went through your head, Raven?"

Nathaniel was looking at me with veiled curiosity, so I told him, and he chuckled, shaking his head. "Would it

58

please you to know that she is afraid of you? Verena laughed her ass off when she heard that one."

Ha! It did please me…it gave me a rush of happy endorphins that I knew when I did kill her, she would know I was her worst fear come to life.

I was suddenly aware that there were only four angels on the ground here, but Nathaniel would never have come here without more League members. If he brought Abraxas with him, I'd shoot the bastard myself.

"You said Verena is back at the citadel. Who else is here?"

Nathaniel arched a brow. "Why do you want to know?"

"Because you landed here for a reason and brought three angels. The three I'd be least likely to order an attack on. You wanted me to be at ease. Had you rocked up with Cassiopeia, Draegan, and Abraxas, things would have gotten violent real fast."

Tiernan glanced at me at the mention of Abraxas, and Nathaniel noticed the movement, looked directly at Tiernan as he said. "I am not so cruel that I would dangle the angel who tried to hurt her in front of her face. I might not be able to kill him, but I take great enjoyment out of making him suffer. However, if Abraxas was to fall by human hands, his death would go unavenged."

I sucked in a breath. Nathaniel had essentially given Tiernan full permission to go after Abraxas, without the fear of repercussion. And by the smile on Tiernan's face, he'd totally accepted that offer. He would go after Abraxas for me…and I wasn't sure I would stop him.

Nathaniel folded his arms across his chest. "Adair and Asterin await above the clouds. I did not know how badly injured you were, so I thought it best to bring Adair."

"It wasn't that bad. I'm grand."

"Two broken ribs. Dislocated shoulder that had to be rebroken and relocated again because Raven thought it would be a fabulous idea to relocate it by running into a wall. Two infected bites from the wastelanders. She fought off the wastelanders with a hurley and then walked the rest of the way here before collapsing."

Both Nathaniel and Adriel were glaring at me. Rolling my eyes, I could have killed Tiernan as I said with a sigh. "He's being dramatic. It wasn't like that."

"It was exactly like that." James commented and I flipped him off.

"Not helping, Superhero."

"I know."

Shaking my head, I didn't know what else to say so I told Nathaniel to call for Adair and Asterin. He lifted his hand in the air, and beckoned with his fingers, and then I heard the beat of wings. There was a stunned silence behind me as petite Asterin landed beside Devika, a second before Adair did, landing right next to his twin. They folded in their wings, Adair scanning me with healer eyes even when I told him I was okay.

Adair's eyes shifted to the man standing to my right, and they widened for a fraction when he recognised Tiernan. I'd only discovered recently that Tiernan had saved Adair's life, almost dying himself in the process and would have, if Adair hadn't of healed him. Adair remembered himself then and turned his focus back on me.

"He is pretty to look at, right?" I said, making Adair laugh which seemed to rile the soldiers behind me up even more. There was a lot of people here that were not happy with how friendly I was behaving toward the monsters they all hated.

"Maybe you could offer some introductions, Raven."

"Don't give me orders, commander. I'm not one of your soldiers."

We glared at each other, fucking electricity in our gazes until Tiernan muttered something under his breath. He didn't say anything though, and it was James who broke the stalemate.

"I'm James, darling. Just don't you forget." He winked at Makata, who was still perplexed by James' flirtations.

"My name is Makata, not darling."

James grinned, then pointed to Tiernan. "He's Tiernan, the one responsible for keeping herself out of trouble."

Adriel snorted and I flipped him off as he said to Tiernan. "That is not an easy task."

"No, it's fucking not." Tiernan grumbled and I growled at him.

One by one, the angels introduced themselves, like Nathaniel felt that humanizing them by using their names would help. I hated to tell him that their distain for angels was deeply ingrained in their DNA. Hell, it was in mine too...and probably why I hated what I was with a passion.

A commotion broke out behind me and the three of us out front went rigid and came to attention. The crowds parted, the battalion shifted, and my mother appeared. She strode forward, her presence commanding, full of authority, and she betrayed no fear.

Eoghan Lynch followed after her like an eager little puppy, but I knew the moment they stepped up beside us, that he had never seen an angel this up close before. He looked just like the recruit had when I thought he might piss himself.

My mother came to stand beside me, and I watched the angels come to some conclusions. Nathaniel's face was unreadable as he looked at us, and then my mother said to me. "Lieutenant Cassidy, make the introductions."

I wanted to tell her to introduce herself, but fucking knew my mother was testing me.

"Lieutenant-general, this is Nathaniel, Commander of the League of Dominious." I would use titles as a way to take away any introduction that sounded like I was over familiar with the angels. "Commander, may I introduce you to Lieutenant-general Róisín Cassidy, the leader of the Rebels." I look Nathaniel dead in the eyes so he might understand things better. "And she's also my mother."

CHAPTER
SIX

A flare of his eyes is the only reaction that gives any indication that Nathaniel is surprised by my introduction. If there was one thing that Nathaniel and me had in common, it was mothers who liked to order us about.

"I would do anything to protect the Imperium. As her soldier and as her son."

That was exactly what Nathaniel had said to me during one of our very first interactions, when he freed me from the prison and put me to work. Maybe now he understood that I would do the same for my mother. Had I not agreed to assassinate the Imperium and sign my own death warrant because she had asked me to?

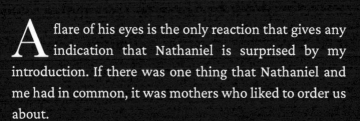

The angels all exchanged glances, and I shifted my gaze to Adriel, who merely tilted his head, and lifted a brow so subtly that no one else would notice. It was a look that said, *you kept that pretty quiet*, and I just gave a slight shrug of my shoulders as if to reply, *would you have said anything if you were me?*

"What brings the commander of the esteemed League of Dominious all the way from the citadel to the Rebel's front door?" My mother asked, folding her arms across her chest, but I knew she could reach for any number of weapons at a second's notice.

Nataniel looked from me to Róisín. "The Imperium upon hearing what had occurred between Raven and Saskia, sent us to ensure that Raven was alive."

I snorted, I couldn't help myself and my mother glared at me. With a sigh, I squared my shoulders and bit down hard on the inside of my mouth not to retort. Nathaniel arched a brow at me and I really, really wanted to go tell him to go fuck himself.

Out of the corners of my eyes, I could see Tiernan and James trying hard not to laugh.

Fucking assholes.

"Perhaps this impromptu meeting could lead to a civilized conversation." Nathaniel broached, trying to play peace maker.

"You're lucky we haven't put a bullet in your head commander. Who the fuck says we want to have a conversation with you fucking monsters." Eoghan spat out, aggression in his tone as he stepped forward, in line with my mother.

Nathaniel looked from Eoghan to my mother, then those eyes full of storms landed on me. "We should talk."

"My daughter does not speak for me, Commander. If

you wish to try and offer some sincerity, then you will speak to me."

Nathaniel was still staring at me as he replied. "I think I'd still prefer to speak to Raven."

Was he trying to get me killed?

I wasn't sure what to do in this situation. I'd always felt like I was being pulled in two directions, one way toward my human DNA and the other toward my angelic DNA. Panic flared in my chest as both my mother and Nathaniel looked at me and I wanted to pull my power to me and disappear.

That would have been fanfuckingtastic except the asshole angel giving me a smug look would still be able to see me.

The moment was broken when a child managed to get passed the battalion, slipped right under Tiernan's legs, and made a beeline for the angels with an awestruck look on her face. I didn't know this child, but she looked like she was maybe three years old.

"Meabh, come back here!" Eoghan shouted, but the child ignored him as she came to a halt before Adair and Adriel.

"Angel!" The toddler held out her hands as if she wanted to be picked up and Adriel took a step back, a sheer look of fear in his eyes.

Adair crouched down, gave the little girl, Meabh, a big smile and her eyes widened. "Hello, little one. I see the Rebels make lots of little girls with no fear in them."

Meabh flung herself at Adair, wrapping her arms

around his neck, and Adair's smile widened. I heard the sound of weapons loading, pointed right at the healer angel as his twin's eyes darkened. Someone with a twitchy trigger finger could take a shot and hurt the little girl if they were not careful.

"Lieutenant-general, Adair is a healer. He could in no way harm the child. It is not in his nature."

My mother arched a brow. "Am I to trust you on this?"

That felt like a kick to the chest. "I would never put a child in harm's way. I know it would cause him distress to hurt someone. If my words are untrue then I offer you my life."

Adair lifted his gaze to mine, and as he got to his feet, the little girl in his arms reached out to pat the top of his wings and Adair didn't so much as flinch, least someone take a shot at him. I shifted my gaze to Adriel, his eyes black with power, though caged, was struggling to get free.

"It is not the so-called healer that causes us concern, Lieutenant. His sibling looks like he wants to eviscerate us all." My mother intoned, and I rubbed my temple, pressure building behind my eyes.

"Well maybe if the firing squad aimed the weapons away from his twin, then Adriel would not feel like his brother's life is in danger." I snarled, my tone coming out as snappy.

Adair pulled a black and green feather from his wing and handed it to the girl. "Might I ask who speaks for this child? I would speak to a guardian."

What the hell was Adair doing?

"I speak for her," Eoghan said, stepping forward again. "The child is my niece."

My head snapped round to Tiernan, who just shrugged. "I forgot to tell you."

Oh ya, it just slipped his mind that while I was gone, Aoife just went and had a child. I had so many questions, who was the father? Was it someone I knew? What else had I missed? Who else had fucking kids that I knew nothing about?

As if sensing my question, Tiernan laughed. "Nope, neither me or James have not made you an aunt, Raven. You can relax."

My mother looked over her shoulder to one of the soldiers, and it amused me that no one had paid any attention to Eoghan trying to claim responsibility for Aoife's kid. "Go and get Sergeant Lynch."

I blinked in surprise. I hadn't even known that Aoife was back on site.

We all stood and watched as Adair chatted to the toddler ignoring the fact that he was already been sized up for his coffin. I made to speak, but my mother told me to stay quiet, so I clamped my mouth shut.

Nathaniel, the prick, gave me a haughty look, as if to say that he wished it was that easy for him to quieten me. The adrenaline in me felt like it was trying to burst out of my skin, making me shift my weight from one foot to the other.

The little girl was pointing at all the things around her like Adair doesn't know what they are, and he listened to her rapt, whispering things and the little girl laughed. The crowd parted and Aoife came striding out, her eyes wide when she spotted her daughter in the arms of an angel.

You would never have recognised her from the woman I had seen in the human servants' quarters a couple of months ago. She was dressed like a civilian, her hair pulled back off her face. She looked like a mother... like how I envisioned mothers looked like before the war.

"Meabh..." Aoife said, moving to go to her daughter, but Róisín stopped her.

"The angel requested to know who spoke for the girl. Let us hear what this healer has to say."

Ah, so that's why my mother was not issuing Adair's death...it was a fucking test to see if I had lied about him being a healer.

My lips curled into a snarl at the realization and my hands clenched into fists at my side. Nathaniel watched me, his gaze narrowing but I dragged my furious gaze from him and my mother and looked at Adair.

His bright green eyes shimmered as he brushed a hand over the top of Meabh's hair. "You are her mother?"

Aoife jerked her head up. "I am."

Adair took a step toward Aoife, making Tiernan advance a step, the two locking gazes before Adair sighed. "I mean her no harm. She is unwell, is she not?"

Now I knew why my mother had been testing both me and Adair. Aoife's daughter was sick, sick enough that no medicine we had could heal her.

Aoife looked at my mother, who gave a slight incline

of her head and then Aoife said. "The doctors say she has a heart condition that could have been healed if we had electricity and a proper surgical team."

Adair offered her a smile full of sympathy. "She has a tiny little hole in her heart that will not repair on its own. It is why also; she has a little rattle in her lungs. She was born early?"

"Ya, six weeks early. It is a miracle she lived as long as she has."

"I can fix it all." Adair said with more confidence than I had ever heard in his tone. "If you would permit it, I can heal her so that she will continue on with life and not only be happy, but healthy also."

Aoife sucked in a breath, her head snapping in my mother's direction. I knew Aoife would be willing to do anything to keep her daughter alive, but it would be *my* mother who would decide if Adair could heal the child or not. I understood the fear in Aoife's eyes because she knew my mother had sent her own daughter off on a suicide mission.

"And why would you heal a rebel's child? What is in it for you?"

Adair shook his head. "There's nothing in it for me only the peace I get from healing. Flying away from here, knowing I could have prolonged her life would eat at me. It is ingrained in me to help others, as a healer." Adair glanced at me with a small smile. "Besides, I'm quite fond of one rebel girl, might as well add another to the collection."

Meabh chose that moment to lean her head on

Adair's shoulder and close her eyes, oblivious to the chaos going on around her. Aoife's eyes pleaded with my mother, and I was about to interject when Adair said,

"I understand the lack of trust. The child is sleeping. You can have one of your soldiers stand with a gun to my head and should I go against my word, a bullet to the head will be a fitting end."

Makata, who had been silent until now, cleared her throat and Aoife looked at her. "I have raised my son on my own since his father was murdered by the Seraphan. I trust each and every angel standing here with his life, but Adair even more so. He would never harm a child, angelic or human."

My mother was watching all the interactions with veiled interest. But it was when Adair spoke again, that a decision was made.

"The child's heart has weakened. The sickness in her heart will not repair as she gets older, only worsen and it will not be able to withstand the changes in her body. We speak in months, not years. Please. Let me heal her."

I think if Aoife could have gotten to her knees and begged my mother she would have, but as noise and commotion started to build behind us, she held up her hand and got complete and utter silence.

"I'll put a bullet in his head if he harms her." Tiernan said, offering when no one else seemed inclined to.

"Please, Lieutenant-general. She will die if he doesn't heal her." Aoife begged, my mother's expression not even changing as she looked to Tiernan.

"If he harms her, you kill him, soldier. That was the bargain struck. He can heal the child and if he reneges no angel or human will stop Tiernan from shooting him. Those are my terms."

Adair's eyes went to Nathaniel, who inclined his head in approval and then Tiernan stepped forward, aiming his shotgun at Adair's temple. Adair ignored the gun, glanced over his shoulder and then back at me.

Adriel was close to losing it. I was stuck between wanting to show my allegiance to the Rebels and protecting my friend. In the end, I huffed out a breath and broke away from the humans, walking right up to Adriel even as my mother ordered me back.

I stood in front of him, then reached out to touch his arm, shivered at the coldness of it.

"Adair's a big boy. He knows what he's doing. I promise you everything will be okay."

I turned and stood with Adriel as Adair closed his eyes, humming a little to the sleeping girl as he placed a hand over her chest and then his eyes sprang open, glowing a little. We stood watching for a few minutes, then Adair blinked, a smile curving his lips.

"Her heart has been repaired. It beats strong and true." Adair stood very still as Aoife came forward, and Adair gently handed the sleeping child to her mother. "She will likely sleep for a time now, as her body adjusts. It is normal. Should you have any worries, I'm sure you can find a way to reach out to me."

Aoife barely held back her tears as she offered a

shocked thank you to Adair then rushed her child back inside the gates, no doubt getting a doctor to assess and see if Adair had in fact healed her. Adair swayed a little, staggered and I made to lunge for him in case he keeled over, but Tiernan swept forward and put a hand out to steady him.

Adair looked at Tiernan, who was looking at Adair like he was a hero or some shit.

"Thank you," Adair said, swallowing hard. "There was a lot of healing needed. I did not want to alarm the mother by telling her as much."

"She's grateful though. It was a kind thing you did."

My mother cleared her throat and Tiernan seemed to remember himself and went back to where he stood, lifting his shotgun upward and at the angels again. I nudged Adriel as if to say, told ya so, then walked back over to stand beside my mother.

"While it remains to be seen if the child is actually healed, this little show of power does not negate anything, nor offers you any sort of amnesty between our species."

Nathaniel tilted his head. "Be that as it may, perhaps there are those amongst your Rebels who have seen what Adair has done and might realize that there could be peace between our people if we engaged in some measure of conversation."

My mother snorted, shaking her head. "I would never have you pegged as an idealist, commander. Your Imperium does not want peace between humans and angels. She is part of the cancer that needs to be cut out.

Her disregard for human life, even now it is my kin who angels use for servants, for fucking, for slaves. Perhaps, we should hold one of you hostage and use as we like, just as your Imperium has used my kin, my daughter."

Róisín let her eyes slide over to Adair. "Perhaps we will keep the healer so that when the Rebels are injured in skirmish with angels, he can heal us over and over."

Adriel stepped in front of Adair, directly in the scope of Tiernan's shotgun. "You would have to go through me to take him and with one thought, one measly little errant thought, I could end all of your lives and not even flinch. It would mean nothing to me."

A lie, I knew, because Adriel did not want to use his powers to kill, making them even stronger than they were. But I knew that the humans wouldn't know that despite the darkness in him, Adriel had a good heart.

And it killed me to know I was betraying him keeping Nathaniel's secrets.

As if my mother had assessed the threat Adriel posed, she smiled. "What is your name, angel?"

"Adriel."

My mother glanced at me, then back at Adriel. "My daughter means something to you."

It was a statement, not a question, as my mother was no doubt recalling what I had told the elders about Adriel stopping Abraxas from raping me. I wanted him to lie, to tell her that I meant sweet fuck all to him, because it would be safer for him if Róisín didn't know that we shared a bond.

"Perhaps." Was all that Adriel said and I almost sagged in relief.

A knowing smile crept over my mother's lips, and my stomach sank. Whatever was running through her head, whatever information she had gleamed from Adriel's response had pleased her.

"Well, now that you all have been assured that Lieutenant Cassidy is no longer in harm's way, you can take your leave. Our good grace I'm afraid is waning."

Nathaniel looked almost bored as he said. "I'm afraid that you are mistaken, Lieutenant-general."

My mother's brows lifted upward. "How so, Commander?"

"We did not come all this way just to see that your daughter was unharmed."

Oh fuck...I knew it...I knew that this would not end amicably.

"While we have already established that Raven did not escape from the citadel, she is still a prisoner of the Imperium. For her crimes of trying to assassinate the Imperium, she was sentenced to death and any reprieve she received does not quash that conviction."

"Of course fucking not," I mumbled, shaking my head, dread pooling in the pit of my stomach. Any semblance of happiness I felt at being home was slowly being ripped away and it fucking hurt.

"What are your intentions, then?" My mother asked.

"We have been sent by the Imperium to retrieve Raven and bring her back to the citadel. She agreed to let us come first to bring her back without bloodshed. If you refuse, if you fight, then we have been ordered to return Raven to the citadel by any means necessary. Raven is to come with us of her own accord or we will take her by force."

SEVEN

There was this moment of utter silence before all hell broke loose. Everyone started talking all at once. James and Tiernan were shouting at the angels to back off, my mother was preparing the battalion to get ready to strike. The angels were taking up defence and attacking positions as Nathaniel withdrew his sword and let a wave of fire coat the blade, the heat of it flushing my skin.

Any goodwill that Adair's healing of the child had done had been evaporated with Nathaniel's stupid fucking declaration. Of course Rieka would want me back. Out here, I was the rebel who not only defied her to her face, but I would become a legend among the Rebels, a defiance of our oppressors.

Forcing me to go back would assure those who might question her right to rule that she was very much still in control. Rieka would have no qualms in killing those I cared about to assert her power, and if they killed

Nathaniel, her only son, then she would raze the humans to nothing but bones.

There was no choice to be made.

I knew that when my eyes clashed with my mother's, and it was as if I could hear her voice in my head. *Your mission is not yet complete.*

"I'll go." I said softly, resigned to my fate.

Tiernan turned to me, shock on his face but he seemed to be the only one who had heard me.

"I'll fucking go!" I screamed, and everything around me halted, every eye on me.

"Raven, no. They don't get to take you from us again." James growled, and I almost sobbed at the emotion in his tone.

"I don't have a choice, James." I told him honestly. "That bitch was never going to let me go. We knew it. I knew it. I thought I'd have more time, but them's the breaks and all that stupid philosophical bullshit."

Nathaniel's fire subsided and he sheathed his sword. "If there was any other way, I would not force you. If we had returned empty handed, then the Imperium would have sent others for you, Raven. I am but the lesser of two evils."

"Every good story needs a villain, and I am sorry if I am the villain in your story."

I ignored him and the memory, turning to face my mother. I saluted her, my stance strong. "Lieutenant-general, I am but a servant of the cause. My mission is still not over, and I offer you what I have always offered in the pursuit of our people. My blood, my body, my life is yours to command."

My mother had never been one to offer any sense that she is proud of me, and I hated that I searched for it in her eyes, disappointment coursing through me when I found none. I think, in this moment, that I finally accepted that she would never be capable of loving me, of being proud of me. I was just another soldier, a weapon in her disposal. And just like Rieka, my value was only in my usefulness.

"This is a decision that you make of your own free will?" my mother asked me, like I had any other fucking choice to make. If I refused to go, innocent blood would be spilled, and I would still end up back in Rieka's clutches.

"It is."

"Then at ease, Lieutenant. Your sacrifice will not be forgotten."

We looked at each other as I dropped my hand, and the little girl in me begged and pleaded for her to show some sort of reaction, to stand here in front of the angels, in front of the rebel army and show that sending her daughter back into captivity affected her in some way.

"Grant them no mercy."

"By your order."

Róisín looked at Nathaniel, the commander glaring at my mother like he could not believe how indifferent she was being toward me. But Nathaniel shouldn't be surprised, I doubted Rieka was the warm and fuzzy kind of mother even when he was a boy.

No, Nathaniel had not learned kindness from Rieka... but from Kalila.

I had Tiernan for that. James too.

"I would advise that you take your leave soon. I doubt we will meet on such friendly terms again, commander."

Nathaniel shrugged. "We could have. But perhaps under new leadership, peace talks would be more... amicable."

My mother scoffed. "Perhaps."

That was all she said as my mother turned, strode back inside the gates, Eoghan again following after her and leaving me outside with the angels and my brothers. My shoulders sagged as the gates closed, and I closed my eyes.

I didn't want to go. I wanted to stay here with these two idiots.

"I'll go with you."

My eyes snapped open at the sound of Tiernan's voice. He looked determined, like he wasn't going to listen to reason, and I loved him even more for it. James nodded his head, like he was planning on coming too.

"Tiernan, no," I said with a sigh, wondering how I could stop either of them. "Even if you two weren't two of the most recognisable Rebels in all of Ireland, if either of you came, it would just give Rieka someone to hurt to get to me. I need to go alone. I have to."

Tiernan held my gaze for a long, tense moment as James ground out. "I fucking hate this. I fucking hate that we just got you back and now we are losing you all over again. Goddammit."

There was heat behind my eyes as I looked to Nathaniel. "Can I have some time to say goodbye?"

"Of course."

I went to James first. He reached out and dragged me into his arms, and I wrapped my arms around his back. We just stood there for the longest time, as James cursed and mumbled. Then he stepped back and grabbed my shoulders.

"This isn't fucking goodbye. You pulled that shit once and then rocked up half dead on our front door. Your Ma might be a cold bitch to hand you back over to them, but I'm making it clear that I am not okay with this. I am not fucking okay."

I reached up and rested my hands on James's arms. "I know. I'm not okay with this either. But I managed to stay alive when everyone thought I'd be long dead. You and Tiernan taught me well, Superhero. I will never stop trying to come home to ye."

James held my gaze. "This isn't goodbye."

"This isn't goodbye."

James swore then yanked me to him again. When he finally let me go, he brushed his knuckles against my cheek. "Give um hell, little sister."

I laughed, the sound coming out more of a sob, as I turned away from James and at Tiernan. He was glaring at me, because this was the third time that he would have to say goodbye to me. He loved me, I knew that as sure as I knew anything else as I walked toward him.

"Don't, I'm not losing you again. I can't." Tiernan said, emotion thick in his voice.

"You aren't losing me, Tiernan. You know where I'll be and I'm sure the commander will tell you if that changes." I looked to Nathaniel. "Can you promise him that? If I die, you will find some way to let them know?"

Nathaniel's jaw clenched, but he nodded his head. "I will find a way."

"He doesn't have to promise me shit because you are not leaving without me, Trouble. Not happening."

Tiernan really wasn't going to make this easy for me, was he?

"You know that can't happen. There are people behind those gates who need you more than I do. They look up to you, they follow your lead. As much as I want to keep you for myself, I can't be selfish, Tiernan. I love you. It would break me if Rieka used you against me. I can withstand everything she throws at me if I know you and Superhero over there are safe. Please. You have to let me go."

"I did that the last time and you were tortured and almost raped." He growled, shoving his hand through his hair.

"Almost, Tiernan. It was only almost because of the training you gave me. Not just that but you gave me a family, a reason to fight. To survive. Coming home has only enforced that. I meant what I said. I will never stop trying to come home to ye. Isn't it better now knowing I'm alive."

Tiernan shook his head. "No. Because I know that

where you are, trouble is not far away. You are reckless, with no thought for your own mortality."

"You're just listing some of my best qualities there."

Tiernan looked like he was ready to say more but I just crashed into him, breathing him in as I mumbled. "I'll ask him to bring me to you again. I'll beg if I have to. For you I'd beg him."

Tiernan's arms go around me and I can't stop the tears or the sobs that wrack my body. He holds me for the longest time, neither of us wanting to be the first to let go. In the end, it's Tiernan that steps back and he cups my face in his hands.

"You stay alive, you hear me." He orders, his thumbs brushing away the last of my tears.

My heart aches. I don't want to fucking go. I miss him already and this time, I think it will be harder to be separated from him and James. I'd gotten used to being without them and it was a new breed of torture, to dangle them in front of me only to have to walk away.

"Raven, promise me that you will stay alive."

I looked into his blue eyes. "I promise to try. I can only promise to try."

Tiernan's expression looked like he was seconds away from grabbing me and dragging me back inside the gates of the barracks. Instead, he turned, looking not at Nathaniel but at Adriel. Their gazes were locked, and my stomach sank at what might happen next.

Though I wasn't expecting what Tiernan said.

"She trusts you, so I do. I'm leaving her in your care. I know she makes it hard, caring about her, but I need to know there is someone looking out for her. Trouble here, she does her best to make it as hard as possible."

"I'm standing right here, you ass." I muttered, but the two men ignored me.

"I am giving you the person who means the most to me in this fucked up world."

Adriel stepped forward, though he did not reach out to Tiernan. "I understand. I will do my utmost to ensure her safety. But as you say, she makes it hard to keep watch over her."

"All I can ask is that you try." Tiernan said with a resigned sigh.

"And I will. You have my word."

I rolled my eyes, kicked at the dirt. "You two sound like you are discussing my dowery or some shit. I can look after myself. I don't need you two talking about me like I'm not even here."

Tiernan glanced over his shoulder to me and grinned. "I don't think there would be a dowery large enough to convince any man to take you on."

Nathaniel snorted and I pointed a finger at him. "You can shut up. Make one smart remark and I will kick you in the nuts."

The commander held up his hands in surrender, but he was grinning. I looked back at James and Tiernan, felt like I was gonna cry all over again. This sucked, this bloody sucked.

"How about a goodbye kiss before I go, darling?" I heard James drawl, looked over to see Makata starring at him. "You could call it a gesture of goodwill between human and angel. I promise you'll enjoy it as much as I would."

Makata flushed a vicious shade of pink, spreading her wings out and taking to the sky, Asterin and Devika following her. James watched her go with a male smugness on his lips, and wonder in his eyes. He felt me looking at him, grinned over at me.

"She's an angel dumbass. You can't have sex with her." I said sharply, ignoring the way Nathaniel was looking at me.

James grinned harder. "I'll try anything once. With her, maybe twice."

I placed my hand on my temples and rubbed. Horny fucking bastard.

I gave the angels my back, then looked at my brothers. "Okay, I'm asking you both to go back inside and let me go without the pain of knowing you are watching as I walk away. I don't think I can do it if you are standing here."

Tiernan shook his head. "You can't walk away from us, but you are asking us to do the same?"

"Well, since I'm the one being carted off to face the Imperium, I think that gives me the bigger pull here." Tiernan and James frowned at me. "Come on. Please? Go back inside."

They both came forward one last time, the three of us hugging, and I whispered. "Do not let Hayes go back to the citadel. It will get him killed. He will get himself killed."

Tiernan kissed my forehead and I saw the turmoil in

85

their eyes. I turned back to face the angels, felt wetness on my cheeks as I slammed my eyes shut, heard the heavy cadence of their footsteps as they did what I asked and went back behind the gates.

I kept my eyes closed long after I heard the gates slam shut, taking a piece of my heart with them. This was the most vulnerable I'd ever been in front of the angels, and I didn't want to see their sympathy, I didn't want to look at them when they were taking me away from my family.

Strong arms went around me, and I bristled, not wanting Nathaniel anywhere near me and was almost relieved when I hear Adair whisper. "It's just me. It's just me. I'm sorry."

I let Adair hold me then I patted him on the arm, and we separated, the healer's eyes shimmering with concern.

"Thanks."

"No hassle." Adair said in a very impressive Cork accent that made me splutter with laughter.

I knew that I must have looked a mess, my face all blotchy from crying, my eyes sad and tired, and I shivered against the cold and loneliness that was sinking into my bones.

"Raven."

Adriel's voice drew my attention, and I looked over to see him throw my jacket, the one he'd gotten me for my birthday at me. I caught it, then slipped my arms into it, instantly feeling warm. I offered him a smile in thanks.

"Coulda done with this in the wastelands. Thanks, Adriel."

Shifting on my feet, I looked back at the gates one last time before I turned to the angels, rolled my shoulders and crossed my arms across my chest. "Right, I suppose we should get going then? It's a long walk back to the citadel."

Adair snorted, as Nathaniel smiled at me like I had said something very fucking amusing. "We are not walking back to the citadel, Raven."

"Well how the fuck do you expect me to get there then, bird boy." I snapped angerly at him, but that made him smile even more so now I wanted to throat punch him.

"We will fly of course," Nathaniel told me, and if I was not mistaken, his voice had gone husky and low.

"Oh hell no. Not happening. Not a chance."

"That's not what you said before, Raven."

"Take me higher."

I remembered the rush I'd felt when Nathaniel had taken me flying.

"Do you want to go back?"

"Not just yet. Can we just fly a little longer. Please."

And I remembered the kiss that had been seared into my memories... that almost had the two of us naked and unable to walk it back.

Nathaniel let out a frustrated growl and his lips crashed into mine. His kiss kindled a flame that had lain dormant inside me until him. His teeth bit down on my bottom lip and I gasped, allowing him to thrust his tongue inside my mouth.

The groan that rumbled from his chest and throat was enough to make me quiver.

Nathaniel walked forward, until my back hit the wall and still, he didn't stop devouring my mouth like he was afraid that if we stopped, even for a second, I would call a halt to this eruption. I pulled my power around us, feeling brave and daring as I yanked his tee from out of his combats and trailed my hands up his muscular frame.

My cheeks felt flush as I shook my head, and from the heated expression Nathaniel was wearing, he too was remembering the kiss. Rolling my eyes, I wet my lips, watched as Nathaniel's eyes traced the movement, and looked at the twins.

"Right, well, if I'm not allowed to walk back to the citadel, then which of you is flying me?"

Adair looked from me to Nathaniel and back again. "I am not getting in between whatever you two have going on. See ya up there."

Adair took off and I yelled coward at him, the wind carrying his laughter right back at me. I looked to Adriel, his face unreadable as he shrugged and then followed his brother.

"Fucking traitor!" I yelled, frustration making out in a growl.

I heard a chuckle, angled my body to face Nathaniel.

"You could at least have the decency to look less smug." I told him.

"It's amusing you think me capable of being decent." Came his tart response, making me want to punch him again.

When I didn't respond, he arched his brow. "You remember that I am in control when we fly."

"Ifyoufuckingsayso." I grumbled, earning me another chortle of laughter, making me dig my heals in and stay rooted to the spot.

"Come closer, Raven."

"Bite me, bird boy."

Nathaniel strode over, halted just an inch from me. Our eyes were locked in a battle of wills, each of us wanting the other to look away first. I could feel the thrum of tension in his body.

It echoed the one in mine.

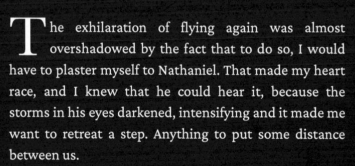

T he exhilaration of flying again was almost overshadowed by the fact that to do so, I would have to plaster myself to Nathaniel. That made my heart race, and I knew that he could hear it, because the storms in his eyes darkened, intensifying and it made me want to retreat a step. Anything to put some distance between us.

Nathaniel didn't have the same thoughts as I do though. His hand reached up and tucked a stray strand of hair behind my ear. I suppressed a shiver, especially when Nathaniel's hands clamped down on my hips. Not giving me any chance to argue with him, he lifted me, and I instinctively wrapped my legs around his waist, and locked my hands around his neck.

Our eyes clashed and I ducked my head, burying my face in the crook of his neck. I felt his shoulders move, his wings rustling, and then the sound of those glorious wings beating as he took to the skies, but not before he locked an arm around my waist.

Once we were airborne, I lifted my head and looked around to see everyone else flying along with us. A sharp pain in between my shoulder blades made me bite down hard on the inside of my mouth. Adair flew closer and asked if I was alright, but all I could do was nod, though he looked at me like he didn't believe me.

I glanced down, saw the faint outline of Cork City as we flew, and I wondered if this would be the last time that I got to see my home. I had left a massive piece of my heart behind me, and I already missed them with every fibre of my being.

"I'm sorry that we had to come so soon."

Nathaniel's voice interrupted my thoughts, and I didn't reply, just ignored him.

"I tried to delay as long as possible, I promise you." Nathaniel continued, his fingers brushing up along my side, making my body heat, and my anger even more so. I hated that I was attracted to him, that his touch made me want to forget everything that divided us. "But once we had your exact location, there was no way I could persuade her to wait even one more day."

I pressed my lips together in a firm frown, holding back my snippy retort, and I heard Nathaniel sigh. He didn't say anything for the longest time, the wind making me shiver despite the jacket Adriel had given me, or maybe it was the heat of Nathaniel's body pressed against me.

"I almost lost my mind when we couldn't find you..."

Nathaniel said softly, his voice nothing more than a whisper in my ear. "Come on, Raven. You will have to speak to me at some point."

I rolled my eyes even though I knew he couldn't see me. For fuck sake why did I have to be flown by him? I would totally kick Adriel's ass in our next training session for blowing me off and forcing me to be stuck with Nathaniel the entire journey back.

When we flew over the wastelands, I shuddered, locking my legs tighter around Nathaniel's waist and I heard him swear under his breath. Well, looked like having me stuck to him like an octopus wasn't only affecting me. His breath was warm against the skin at my throat, and I didn't want to look at his face to read his expression.

I shifted slightly, my ribs still a little sore and my shoulder was starting to ache. I was tired and sad, and in that moment, a small part of me would have preferred to plummet to the ground and just end it all. I was just so tired of being a pawn in everyone's twisted fucking game. I was sick of being Nathaniel's gambit, I was sick of being Ricka's pet rebel, and I was sick of being looked at like a traitor.

Panic flared in my chest, and I heard Nathaniel ask me if I was okay.

When I didn't respond, Nathaniel snarled, then dove downward. Wind whipped around me, and Nathaniel landed on the ground so hard that he sank into the muddy grass. I untangled myself from him, but he held his arm around my waist until I shoved at his chest.

When he let me go, I walked away from him, strode right into the middle of the woods that he had landed in and opened my mouth. The scream that came out of me wasn't exactly human, my fists clenched by my sides as I tried to empty myself of all the goddamn pain I was feeling.

I only stopped screaming when a hand landed on my good shoulder. Anger flooded through my veins, and I whirled, aiming my fist for Nathaniel's face. He blocked me, his expression unreadable, as I continued to come at him. I kicked out, not with any finesse or anything, but just looking for an outlet for my pain.

"Talk to me, Raven."

There is a slight undercurrent of an order in his tone, and it just plucks at the taunt strings of my anger. "Go fuck yourself, bird boy. You can take one of those branches and shove it so far up your ass you get splinters in your mouth!"

Nathaniel growled, snapping out his hand to grab me by the throat. The heat in his palm had nothing to do with his power, but from the anger and fucking smoulder in his eyes. I smacked at his arm, but he didn't budge as he walked me back toward a tree.

My back slammed into the hard trunk, and I kicked out. My attempt was halted by a muscular thigh between my legs, holding me in place and I lifted my gaze to meeting the storm clouds that was Nathaniel's gaze.

I have just enough time to take a breath before Nathaniel's mouth was on mine. His lips crashed against mine, devouring my mouth with a fever that stemmed from him and transferred to me. His hand was still on my throat and it both infuriated and thrilled me. Nathaniel kissed me like he was dying, and I was the oxygen he needed to survive.

He groaned when I bit down hard on his lower lip, the sound vibrating throughout my entire body and then he moaned, and I realized that I was moving my hips, sliding my core against his thick thigh. From the hardness pressed against my stomach, Nathaniel was enjoying himself too.

His hand moved from my throat to travel down my body. I wanted to complain about the absence of it, but Nathaniel tore his lips from mine, both of us breathing hard. His lips brushed against my cheek, my jaw, then he sucked on my throat, hard enough to mark and I threw my head back. The moan that came out of me didn't even sound like me.

Nathaniel's tongue licked over the spot he had bitten, and my hips bucked, the combination of his thick thigh and the friction of his pants against me had me wet and searching for release.

Fuck, if Nathaniel made me come and he'd barely touched me, I'd never live it down.

I needed to put a halt to this right damn now.

My hands reached between our bodies, I fumbled for his belt loop, and Nathaniel said my name in a husky tone. I couldn't get his belt open, and that made me snarl, and when Nathaniel chuckled in my ear as he bit my earlobe, I snarled again and cupped him through his pants.

His chuckle faltered as he swore, capturing my mouth in another blistering kiss that felt inhuman, claiming, and something we couldn't come back from. Nathaniel shifted his hand to cup my breast, his palm almost covering it, and then as he moved his thigh back and forth in rhythm with my hips, he pinched my nipple.

My body erupted, like a volcano, and I cried out, unsure if I said his name, or what, my head slamming against the tree. Shudders wracked my body, and I swear stars winked behind my eyes. I rode the waves as Nathaniel kissed my skin, his hands skimming my body until I stopped shaking.

Nathaniel stopped moving, and his chest was heaving like he was struggling to breath, just like I was. Bravely, or possibly stupidly, I lifted my gaze to his expecting to see smugness, but instead, I saw a guarded expression, like he was expecting me to lose my shit and accuse him of taking advantage.

"Why are you stopping?" I asked him, my voice husky, and I told myself it was from, the screaming.

Nathaniel shook his head, removing his thigh from between my legs, and taking a step back. "It is for the best."

I blinked in surprise. Nathaniel had been the one forcing this attraction between us. He was the one who had been all for us getting naked and now he was pulling back? What the fuck?

"Right, sure. For the best. Gotcha." I said, as I righted my clothes, hating how the ache between my legs reminded me that I wanted him to fuck me against the tree.

Ducking my head, I stalked off, heard Nathaniel swear behind me and then his heavy bootsteps as he came after me and grabbed my arm. I whirled round to face him, wanting to yank my arm away but he had taken hold of my still sore one, and yanking it away might just dislocate the bloody thing again.

His lips slammed into mine in a hard, firm, and all too fleeting kiss, before he rested his forehead against mine. "You are so angry right now. With me, with your mother, with my mother. You want something to take away all the pain you feel and as much as I crave to take you, fucking you against a tree is not what I have been fantasizing about. I want to take my time with you, Raven."

I swallowed hard, knowing that he was right. Wasn't that what I had done with Hayes? I had gone to his bed, knowing he wouldn't refuse me, wanting to feel alive when I was facing my death. That had been an unmitigated disaster. And now I was using Nathaniel to forget my sadness and my anger.

I was ashamed of myself.

My thoughts must have been crystal clear on my face because Nathaniel grabbed my hand and placed it over his erection. I hissed, tried to snatch my hand back.

"Never doubt that I want you, Raven. Body and soul, all of me fucking wants you."

Nathaniel let my hand go and I stalked away to put some distance between us. My shoulder ached, and I reached up to rub it. I felt exhausted and emotional, and the last thing I want to do is start blubbering in front of Nathaniel.

"Is your shoulder still sore?" Nathaniel asked me.

"Ya, a little. Ribs too. I think I've gone soft. Becoming too reliant on Adair."

Nathaniel chuckled. "I know it would have meant a lot to him, what you did and said back at the Rebel base. That you trusted him with the child."

I shrugged, then sat down on the grass, my back against a tree. "I know now that Adair doesn't have a malicious bone in his body. He could kill me to protect someone he cared for, but it would change him. Not as much as it changed Adriel, mind. Adair would lose the optimism he has and there are far too many cynical people in this world."

Nathaniel lowered himself to the ground in front of me, stretching out his long legs and leaning back on his arms. "Your brothers love you."

"Ya, well, the feeling is mutual. Even if the idiots drive me mad sometimes."

Nathaniel smiled but didn't say anything and I sighed. "You'll reach out to Tiernan if I die, right? Just like I asked?"

"I gave my word. And though you might not believe me, I do try and keep my promises."

I don't say anything to that, just close my eyes before I venture. "Feels weird that you've met me mam now."

"It helps me understand you a little bit more. We

share similar, what is it you would say, bitches for mothers."

I laughed then opened my eyes. "That's true. I'm lucky I had Tiernan and James to care about me. I'd hate to think what I would have become if I only had her influence when I was growing up."

Nathaniel picked up a blade of grass and rolled it between his fingers. "I am grateful for the time that I had with my father. He was a great father and a true warrior. A leader everyone could have followed. I often wonder if he had been alive when we came to this world, if things would have been different."

He tilted his head to look at me. "Do you ever wish that your mother had been less cold?"

Nathaniel might have asked me the question, was awaiting my answer, but I could tell from his tone that he wished that Rieka had been less cold toward him. Róisín and Rieka were more alike than I cared to admit, and I can't help but think of what Nathaniel had said to my mother back at the barracks.

"I would advise that you take your leave soon. I doubt we will meet on such friendly terms again, commander."

Nathaniel shrugged. "We could have. But perhaps under new leadership, peace talks would be more...amicable."

My mother scoffed. "Perhaps."

Had Nathaniel been hinting at a change in leadership for the angels? And if so, would Nathaniel be the one to assume the position of Imperium? I hadn't been lying when I told Tiernan that the soldiers looked up to him, and if my mother was usurped by Tiernan, could there finally be peace?

I snorted, hating myself for thinking that because I certainly was not a fucking optimist. Life had ripped that emotion from my chest and stomped all over it. I was truly a pessimist, expecting the worst, and never being surprised when things just were shittier.

Nathaniel was looking at me expectantly, and I thought about his question for a few minutes before I gave him an honest answer. "I don't know. Had my mother been like a proper mam, then it might have made me soft and soft doesn't survive in this world. The boys showed me love, but they also showed me how to survive. It was Tiernan who broke my first bone so I would know what it felt like to be tortured, but it was also Tiernan who hugged me when I cried the first couple of times."

A growl rumbled in Nathaniel's chest.

"No, don't be angry. It was a blessing compared to what the elders put me through growing up and when they figured out I had a power, they were almost gleeful."

"It must have been painful to be back there, with the people who hurt you."

"Not as painful as it was to walk away from the ones I love. This time, it feels more final. Like it's the last time. Like I can feel it in my bones."

"I do wish that I did not have to bring you back. If there was any other way, I would have found it."

I don't know why but I believe him. "I know."

We are both quiet for a few minutes, then Nathaniel

looked up toward the sky even though it was blocked by the trees. "Ascian and I, we were like brothers. I was as close to him as you are to Tiernan and James. When Rieka killed my father, he grieved with me. But unlike Tiernan and James, he used my grief to push his mindset on me. I regret all my choices after my father died."

I couldn't imagine Tiernan and James manipulating me like Ascian had done to Nathaniel, or how hurt I would feel if I found out that they had. I toed Nathaniel's boot and gave him a soft smile.

He snorted, running a hand through his hair. "Would you scold me if I told you that it highly amused me when you put that soldier back in his place? The human from the citadel truly looked like he wanted to put that bolt through my chest."

"I know it amused you, I could see it and so could he."

"The soldiers respect you. It was enlightening to see you as a soldier..."

"And not a prisoner or a tool?" I retorted with a snort and Nathaniel frowned.

"That's not what I meant. You had your usual swagger but more."

I pushed off the ground and got to my feet. "They fear me. Even some of the elders fear me."

"A healthy dose of fear among those you command sometimes is not a bad thing, Raven. I saw respect among the soldiers. Though the boy is clearly in love with you."

I ignored Nathaniel's comment on Hayes' feelings toward me, sighing as I said. "I was a child, Nathaniel, when they forged me into a weapon. When they beat me until I couldn't stand yet still forced me to get the fuck back up."

"They trained you to fight and win. You have done so many a time."

Raven snorted. "Ya, they did a great job. And they built it so that most of the soldiers are afraid of me, afraid of what I can do without my power. But they were right to fear me. There is a darkness in me, one that terrifies even me sometimes."

Nathaniel opened his mouth to respond, the flap of wings making him get to his feet as Devika landed on the ground, looked from me to Nathaniel, a stupid grin on her face as she said. "If you two aren't about to fuck each other's brains out, then maybe we can get moving? It will be night soon and I'm starving."

Before I can even tell Dev to fuck right off, she takes to the skies again with a chortle of laughter. Nathaniel doesn't say anything in response, just walks over to me and lifts me so that we are in the same position that we were prior to our descent. Being this close reminds me of what happened against the tree and once more my body is eager and willing to repeat the action.

"You'll be the fucking death of me, Raven." Nathaniel mumbled against my ear and before I can respond, we are shooting upward and heading back toward the citadel.

And that doused the flames of lust curling in my stomach.

CHAPTER
NINE

W e landed in the citadel about an hour later, landing in the courtyard and my legs felt a little unsteady. Exhaustion swept through me and all I wanted was to crawl into bed and sleep. After I gave Grainger a pat or two. I yawned, rubbing my eyes but I could see that all the angels looked solemn, and uneasy.

I was on edge as my eyes landed on Adriel and he looked pissed. The doors to the courtyard burst open, and Kalila came rushing toward me. I had only a second to brace before her arms were around me, hugging me so hard she shoved the air from my lungs.

"Oh my word," she said, her tone sounding like she was close to tears. "I was so worried."

"I'm okay. But my ribs are still sore."

"I'm so sorry!" Kalila exclaimed as she let me go to glare at Adair. "Why have you not healed her?"

I wanted to speak up for Adair, but the healer only laughed as he came to stand beside me. "There was little

103

time. I healed a small child who was gravely ill and needed to retain some strength to fly back. I will heal her now if she would allow it."

I shook my head. "I can wait. You did too much today. I'll be grand after a proper night sleep. You can work your magic tomorrow."

Adair looked like he was about to argue, but then Adriel came over and Kalila ducked her head. Adriel chuckled, and I looked between the two of them. "Okay, what happened here?"

"Nothing..." Kalila replied, her cheeks flushing pink. "I was worried about you."

"So much so that she not only slapped Saskia when she found out what she had done to you, she also slapped me for not telling her the truth."

My eyes widened at Kalila, and she looked at the ground. "I forgot myself. I do not regret slapping Saskia though. I will not apologise for that."

I laughed, so hard my ribs protested a little. "Oh I would have paid good money to see that."

"I feared the Imperium would reprimand me for my actions."

My laughter halted and my gaze narrowed before I asked, my tone deathly cold. "Did she?"

Kalila shook her head vigorously, then I heard Nathaniel say behind me. "I would not have allowed Kalila to be punished for her actions. Saskia was lucky I did not throttle her myself."

Well, thank Christ for small mercies.

I looked at Kalila, whose pale blue eyes watched me,

then said. "You should let the League give you some lessons. Next time, you can punch Sparkles and do some real damage."

Kalila shook her head. "Oh no, I did not like myself after I was violent. Master Adriel already offered his services, to which I politely declined."

I glanced at Adriel, who just shrugged. "I had the same thought as you."

I grinned, but that quickly changed to a yawn. "Right, I'm fucking wrecked so I'm going to bed. You guys can catch me up on everything in the morning or whatever."

All the angels looked at Nathaniel as he held my gaze. "We were ordered to bring you to see the Imperium upon your return. Once she has seen that you are back, then you can sleep."

Arching my brow, I crossed my arms across my chest, too bloody tired and annoyed to be diplomatic. "And if I refuse?"

"Don't refuse."

Rolling my eyes, I pivoted and headed for the door, striding into the League's living area and heading for the corridor that would bring me to the goddamn Imperium. Of course, Rieka would want to delight in having me back under her control. She would be smug as fuck the moment I was presented to her and want to rub it in my face.

It would be a victory to her...

And that pissed me off.

I felt Nathaniel at my back, knew he and probably

one or two more angels were coming to make sure that I didn't do anything to annoy Rieka too much. I was about to turn around and tell Nathaniel I didn't need any babysitters when the door to one of the rooms opened and Verena stepped out, a dejected Saskia following her out.

Saskia's wings had been chopped off; the musculature exposed. Small bursts of feathers had started to grow back, but there was no way she was flying with those wings. Her skin was pale, bruises under her eyes from lack of sleep.

Her hair was knotted, and she looked like utter shite. She was even wearing an unflattering t-shirt that feel over her frame, masking any semblance of the curves I knew she wielded like weapons.

Verena's eyes widened when she saw me, saw us, and she looked like she wanted to shove Saskia back into the room as if we hadn't seen her. Nathaniel swore behind me. Anger bubbled in my veins, and I wanted to make Saskia bleed for what she had done to me. I wanted to hurt her...I wanted her dead.

Saskia lifted her head then, her lips curling into a snarl at the sight of me. I turned away from her, saw Nathaniel breathe a sigh of relief that I wasn't going straight for violence. He was wrong. I was already reaching for the axe at Nathaniel's waist when I heard Saskia mutter loud enough for everyone to hear her.

"Like a cockroach. She's like a fucking cockroach. You just can't kill her."

The axe was in my hand before Nathaniel had a

chance to react and I yanked my power to me. Nathaniel tried to grab for me, but I ducked, heading straight for Saskia. Verena shouted at Nathaniel to tell her where I was, however before Nathaniel could give a clear directive, I had Saskia by the throat.

I shoved her at the door she had just come out of with such force that the door broke, and I heard Saskia whimper in pain. She couldn't see me, but she tried to slap at me. Anger fuelled me as I let go of her throat, tossed her to the ground before I dropped to straddle her chest.

Drawing on my power a little more, I wrapped it around us, shielding us from view from everyone bar Nathaniel. Saskia hissed at me, stilling when she felt the blade of my axe kiss her throat. At this angle, even if anyone tried to knock me off her, I'd still slit her throat.

It might just be worth the repercussions to watch her bleed out under the blade of my axe.

"How the fuck do you keep surviving? How the fuck do you keep managing it?"

I let my lips curve into a smug smile. "I am just that good, Saskia. Something that you will never be, and I can understand why Nate dumped your ass. Who wants to fuck a weak ass bitch when he could be fucking a warrior?"

Saskia hissed at me like a cat, and I laughed, even more so when she sneered. "I can smell him on you. Your luck will run out soon, you human fucking rat, and I'll laugh my ass off when they are crying because you are dead. Abraxas is gunning for you. I might watch while he fucks you to death."

The thought of Abraxas being anywhere near me made me sick to my stomach but I wasn't about to let Saskia see that.

"Threaten me all you want, Sparkles, but I'm the one with the axe to your fucking throat."

"Raven."

I ignored Nathaniel's warning tone as I leaned in closer to Saskia. "I heard you've been spending some quality time with Verena. I heard that your biggest fear was me. You should fear me, Sparkles. If you make it out of here alive, just remember I can sneak into your filthy fucking bedroom and kill you while you are sleeping or being fucked like a whore. Everyone will know it was me but never be able to prove it. Assuming anyone even cares enough to check."

Saskia squirmed under me like she was gonna try and buck me off, but I pressed the blade a little harder into her flesh, just enough to nick her skin and make her bleed.

"I'll kill you, you fucking bitch. I'll kill you!"

I laughed, shaking my head. "You tried, remember? You had your chance to kill me but you failed. Besides, I've seen scarecrows with more spine than you."

Saskia howled in frustration, and that made me laugh even harder.

"Enough, Raven. You've made your point."

"No, Nate. I haven't even begun to make my point." I snapped in response to his chastising tone.

"If you kill her, then she doesn't get to suffer. But you will. The Imperium will punish you for killing her and revoke your freedom. Or worse."

I tilted my head like I was contemplating his words, though in this moment, I didn't care about any consequences. Saskia would keep coming for me if I didn't show her that she couldn't best me. Abraxas would keep coming for me if he believed that I would back down simply on Nathaniel's word.

"Grant them no mercy."

Glancing over my shoulder, I scanned the angels that were now in the room, then looked back at Saskia. She was smirking at me like she knew I wouldn't hurt her because I was afraid of what might happen to me. Like it mattered to me that she was in Rieka's favour, and that Saskia believed that Rieka would avenge her if I did something to her.

Stupid fucking bitch.

I remembered the fear I'd felt freefalling from the sky, hitting the ground and the pain as my shoulder dislocated. The terror I'd felt when I thought I'd not be able to kill all the wastelanders and get out alive. Saskia had made me feel all those things because she was jealous.

She didn't deserve my sympathy.

She deserved to fear me.

Letting go of the hold I had on my power, I brought us back into view. I could tell from the look in her eyes that she was relieved, especially when someone who I presumed was Nathaniel took a step closer to us.

I looked Saskia dead in the eyes as I smiled and

109

leaned forward to press my lips against hers. "Kiss for good luck." I muttered against her lips, echoing her final words to me before she dropped me from the sky.

Her eyes widened as I slid the blade of the axe across her throat in one swift movement. Saskia tried to scream but it came out in a gurgle, and I rolled off her to stand over her as she clutched at her throat, blood coating her hands.

Nathaniel roared for Adair as I watched the panic in Saskia's eyes. Nathaniel dropped to his knees to press his hands to her throat. He called for Adair again, the healer hesitating in the doorway even as Nathaniel snarled.

Adair glanced to me, and I shrugged, showing him I didn't care. Then he moved, dropping to the other side of Saskia, smacking Nathaniel's hands away and I felt his power flowing as he healed Saskia.

"Hand me the axe, Raven."

Without so much as glancing at Adriel, I handed him my axe, then stepped back until I hit the wall. I could see Verena watching me, but I was smiling as Adair took his hands off Saskia, and the bitch was whole again. She sobbed, reaching for Nathaniel, but he rose, ignoring her cries.

Nathaniel glared at me for a moment, then shifted his gaze to Verena. "Take Saskia to her room to get cleaned up. Stay with her. Take someone else with you. Keep her confined to her room and do not, under any circumstances let her speak to Abraxas."

Verena came forward, ordering Saskia to her feet. The angel did, her lips curving into a snarl as she opened her mouth to speak and Nathaniel's growl was so inhuman, the hairs on my arms raised and I held back a shiver.

"Do not speak. Do not so much as open your goddamn mouth, Saskia or I swear I will hand Raven back her axe and walk out of this room and lock you inside with her. Alone. And Adair will not be saving your life a second time round. Now fucking move."

When she still didn't make to move, Verena dragged Saskia from the room, and I watched as Nathaniel turned his glare on Adair. I was conscious that Adriel was standing beside me, felt his body tense. Adair lifted his gaze to Nathaniel and held his stare for a heartbeat before he looked away.

"Who is your commander, Adair?"

"You are, sir." Adair answered, a little movement in his wings the only indication that he was unnerved.

"Then you do not look to others when I give you a direct order."

Ah so Adair was being chastised for looking to me.

"To be fair, you didn't even give him an order."

"Raven," Adriel warned me, but I ignored him and continued with Nathaniel glaring at me.

"What actually happened was you called his name, twice, however you never gave him a direct order. It might have been implied...but maybe Adair didn't understand what you wanted, Nate."

If Nathaniel could have burned me from where he stood, I'm pretty sure he would have.

"Not helping, Raven." Adair muttered and I laughed,

trying to keep Nathaniel's attention on me and away from Adair.

"What? Like it's not true. Besides, I checked to see if Adair was nearby so he could heal the bitch. Though there was a moment, when he hesitated, and I thought she was really gonna bleed out, that really got me feeling all warm and fuzzy."

Nathaniel growled again, and Adair ducked his head as if he was really trying not to laugh. Adriel shook his head, then asked Nathaniel if he wanted my axe back. Nathaniel's eyes bore into me and he arched a brow as if in question.

"Well, since I'm feeling particularly murdery today, probably best if someone else holds onto it since we have one more stop to make on this return leg of the tour. I've got-"

"Poor fucking impulse control...we all remember." Nathaniel snarled, and I just shrugged because it was very fucking true.

I felt him before I saw him, my body going on full alert as I took the axe from Adriel's grasp a lot easier than I expected, and I knew that my friend hadn't made it hard for me to take it. Abraxas' pale blue eyes went straight to me, his tongue flickering out to trace his lips. Nausea rolled in my stomach as he stepped into the room.

"I see you managed to bring the bitch back. I can take her to see the Imperium."

"If you think I'm letting you anywhere near me, Brax,

you're about to add to the blood on the floor." I ground out, ignoring the look on Nathaniel's face.

Abraxas inhaled, closing his eyes for a moment, then he shuddered, like the scent of blood turned him on. Knowing him, it probably did.

"Was it you who made Saskia bleed?"

Jerking my chin up, I gave Abraxas my best *you bet I did* smile. "My axe slipped along her throat like a knife through butter."

Darkness appeared in his gaze, something akin to hunger. "It turned you on, didn't it? Got you all hot and bothered making Saskia bleed?"

I wasn't as depraved as Abraxas, even if I had felt some delight in almost killing Saskia, I would never let Abraxas think we were any way alike. It would only make him fixate on me even more and he already wanted to kill me and fuck me...in what order I wasn't so sure.

"Nah, I felt nothing. It was like swatting a fly that was annoying me by buzzing around my ear."

Abraxas inhaled again. "I can smell how much you enjoyed it, bitch."

Nathaniel snarled and took a step toward Abraxas. Jesus, I felt unnerved to know that Abraxas could smell aspects of my body, even more so that every angel probably could. There was gonna be even more bloodshed if I didn't step in between them. Pushing off the wall, I put a hand on Nathaniel's chest, and looked over at Abraxas.

"What can I say, Nate missed me. I didn't get my rocks off making your fuck buddy bleed, Brax. I got my rocks off because Nate here knows how to drive me insane."

Nathaniel's hand went to cup the back of my neck, and I swear I could almost hear him purring in satisfaction at my admission. There was no taking it back. He squeezed a little harder, and I shivered, hating myself for my body reacting and remembering how I had come alive when his hand wrapped around my throat.

Abraxas sneered, opened his mouth to say something, but Nathaniel shut him down. "Don't start on me, Abraxas. I'm tired and angry and frustrated. I will relish taking some of that frustration out on you. Get out of my sight. That's an order."

He looked like he was going to defy Nathaniel's order, but Abraxas just chortled, before saying to me. "I'll see you soon, Raven."

"Not if I see you first, Braxy. Preferably with a blade to your throat."

"Just the way I wanna fuck you."

Nathaniel snarled, his grip on my neck tightened to the point where it hurt and then Abraxas was gone, and I could hear him laughing as he walked down the corridor. No one moved for a second, then Adriel motioned for Adair to follow him out, leaving me and Nathaniel alone.

"You can let me go now."

"No, I can't." There was an edge to his tone that had me sighing.

"Okay, but you're squeezing too tight. It hurts."

The pressure eased a little, but Nathaniel kept his hand where it was. I knew I'd already pushed too many buttons for him in the space of a few hours, so I stood there, letting him work through whatever he needed to work through.

Maybe it was a little self-preservation.

Maybe I just liked him being possessive.

Maybe I was just royally fucked up in the head.

Maybe, I was just too tired to care in that moment.

I wasn't sure how long we remained in the room, Nathaniel's hand still firmly grasping the nape of my neck. I could *feel* the tension rolling off his body and wondered how close he was to losing his shit. After a long time, his thumb grazed the skin at the side of my neck and I shivered, wishing I could lean back into the heat of him and convince him that a visit to the Imperium was the least fun we could be having tonight.

"You want to tell me what's set you off or are we going to stand here for the rest of the night? I'm tired, Nate. And sore. Flying with damaged ribs is not fun and my shoulder still hurts."

A growl rendered through the room. "If you hadn't been so impulsive then Adair could have healed you. Instead, you not only tried to kill Saskia, but you caused dissent between my League."

I tried to step away from his grasp, felt his hand tighten for a second before the pressure eased again, like

Nathaniel remembered that he didn't actually want to hurt me. His thumb was back to grazing the flesh at the side of my neck.

"That was not on me, Nate. And it wasn't Adair's fault either. The only angel to blame for all of this is your ex. You all treat Adair like he's fragile, but he had a will of steel. If he didn't want to save Saskia, maybe you should ask him why and not just snarl and shit."

I jerked out of his grasp, knowing he could have held me there if he truly wanted. Turning, I hold out my axe, still coated in Saskia's blood, and hand it to Nathaniel. His eyes bore into me as he took the axe, wiped the blood with the end of his top and then sheathed it at his hip.

We glared at each other for a hot second, the anger in his eyes turning to molten heat that had me snapping my gaze away and striding toward the door. Yanking open the door, I saw that Adriel was leaning against the wall, his arms folded across his chest and his eyes closed. I opened my mouth to speak, felt Nathaniel step into the hallway and took an extra step to put some distance between us.

Adriel opened his eyes slowly, the dark green almost black as he looked behind me to Nathaniel. "You'll speak to Adair about what happened. He fears punishment for his actions."

It didn't sound like Adriel was asking Nathaniel, more like telling him what he needed to do, and I glanced over my shoulder to see Nathaniel's gaze narrowing. "Are you giving me orders now, Adriel?"

Adriel let loose an amused snort. "Merely making a

suggestion. He will not sleep if he fears he has disappointed you and his power will be weaker if he has not rested. Next time, he may not have enough to heal anyone that needs healing."

Nathaniel glared for a moment, then grunted, brushing past me and Adriel to stride toward his mother's throne room. I looked at Adriel, the other angel just shrugged, his black and green wings shifting slightly as his shoulders moved. Letting out a sigh, I traipsed after Nathaniel, felt Adriel fall into step behind me, like he was watching my back for any angel who might want to attack me.

That was a very long list.

"Raven!"

I had a second to brace before I was barrelled into, the momentum slamming me hard into the wall, the impact stealing the air from my lungs. My shoulder screamed at me as my vision swam, and nausea rolled in my stomach. Fuck that hurt.

I heard a voice apologize, as I slid down the wall, closing my eyes to stop the fucking room from spinning. I knew Zepher hadn't meant to hurt me, but with the injuries I had, getting run into by a baby angel was as impactful as hitting the ground at full tilt.

Someone said my name, asked me if I was okay, and should they call Adair. I shook my head, then instantly regretted it. I put a hand to my head, inhaling sharply and then let out a pained gasp when a burst of pain stabbed my in the ribs.

I heard crying and knew the young angel must be upset.

"I'm okay, Zepher." I managed to ground out in an even tone. "I was already hurt. I know you didn't mean it. I'll be okay."

Makata must have hauled her son away then because I heard her comfort him as their voices trailed off. I didn't think I could get up without falling over and there was no way in hell was I going to stand in front of Rieka half dead. I wasn't gonna let her see me as weak.

"Raven, open your eyes."

I did as Adriel asked me, looked into eyes that were caught between black and green. "I'm not dead yet."

Adriel chuckled and set his hand down on my knee. I felt a brush of coldness, darkness, like a lick of Adriel's power was checking me out to see if I was close to death and it faded after a quick scan of my body before a different sensation began. Adriel's eyes flashed a luminous green, not unlike his twin's eye colour. Warmth spread from the place where he was touching, making my entire body tingle, and I sucked in a gasp, shocked when it did not hurt, not in the slightest. The warmth was suddenly gone, Adriel scrambling away until his back hit the opposite wall and he was looking at his hands in disbelief.

Had Adriel just healed me?

"That is not possible."

I made to get to my feet, Nathaniel reaching out a hand to help me to my feet, and just in case I wasn't as healed as I thought I was. There was no ache in my ribs. There was no ache in my shoulder. I didn't feel sick or dizzy or anything. In fact, I felt like I could start a fight and fucking throw down without breaking a sweat.

The extent of Adriel's power, life and death, was so powerful that one touch, one tiny touch had healed me when I knew it would have taken Adair minutes if not more to get the same results. I let go of Nathaniel's hand to look down at Adriel.

He was still staring at his trembling hands in disbelief, his face pale, his eyes wide and back to the darker shade of green. I was about to say something, when I felt Nathaniel just tap my shoulder and I stepped back, letting Nathaniel crouch down in front of Adriel.

Nathaniel reached out and grasped one of Adriel's hands in his, causing my friend to shudder. He blinked, then shifted his gaze from his hands to his commander. Nathaniel held his gaze, and then he spoke, I felt goosebumps on my skin.

"For so long, my friend, you have held on to the darkness of what was done to you. It consumed you and it thrived inside of you until all you believed was that death was all you had to offer the world. But what you have done this night is proof that there is still light inside of you. It does not have to be one or another, Adriel. There can be both. Light and dark, they can survive in harmony with one another."

Adriel snatched his hand back, his eyes darting from Nathaniel to me. "You will not speak a word of this."

Nathaniel rose, his wings twitching as he inclined his

head, then Adriel glared at me, and I held up my hands in surrender.

"Hey, it's not my secret to tell. I get it. Some secrets are best left unsaid."

Nathaniel gave me a sharp look, and I rolled my eyes. Oh ya, like I was gonna blurt out all the secrets and lies that Nathaniel was holding on to. Like I was gonna just tell an already freaked out Adriel that his ex was actually a spy for Nathaniel in the Seraphan and they tortured him because Raisel had decided that it might have broken Adair beyond repair.

"Adair must not know. He has thrived in his role as the League's healer and we do not know if this, this thing was just a fluke and the last surge of any healing power I once had. This is something we must not share."

"No one will say anything, Adriel. Now, we must go see the Imperium before she grows more impatient. She would have been advised of our arrival, and will surely already be annoyed as to the time it has taken for us to present ourselves to her. I can take Raven alone if you need a few moments to collect yourself."

Adriel shook his head. "No. We should go."

I put my hands on my hips. "Nah, maybe we should hang around for a few more minutes. Pissing Rieka off seems like a fanfuckingtastic way of ending the night."

Adriel rolled his eyes as he got to his feet, the ghost of a smile on his lips. Nathaniel inclined his head, and we started off again, heading toward the throne room. The scent of food made my stomach grumble, making Nathaniel look at me.

"Don't look at me like that, Nate. I haven't eaten in hours; I've burned calories and I'm starving. Not my fault I have to go see your bitch of a mother before I get fed, so don't look at me like that."

Nathaniel stopped us along the hallway, ducked inside a room and came out with some bread. I could have kissed him for it, chose not to, and munched on the bread as we continued down the hall, finishing up before we reached the door that would lead into the throne room.

Nathaniel turned to face me as I swallowed the last of my bread. "Hold your tongue and this will be over quickly. Let her chastise you. Let her gloat and feel like this is a battle she had won. Please, Raven, do not give her any excuse to publicly punish you for what happened."

Anger seeped into my veins. "This was not my fault. I didn't run away or escape. Saskia kidnapped me and tossed me to the wastelands to die. I didn't do that to myself. For once this is something she actually can't blame me for."

The look on Nathaniel's face told me that she could, and quite obviously was going to. I wished for about the millionth time that my original mission had been a success.

He lifted his closed fist, knocked hard on the door, then opened it to stride in, leaving me to follow, and a silent Adriel coming in behind me. The throne room was almost empty, the evidence of a party still in the room. I knew what kind of parties Rieka liked to host, and the bread in my stomach felt like it wanted to come right back up.

Nathaniel cleared his throat, and his entire body looked like he was fighting his unease. I stepped up beside him, letting my gaze shift to where Rieka was lounging on her throne. Her hair hung loose around her shoulders, the blonde glinting in the candlelight, with her yellow eyes even more so against the darkness of her outfit. She wore a skintight black dress that exposed her long muscular legs and clung to her curves like a second skin. Her arms were covered down to her wrists, the shoulders of the dress had jagged points that looked as if they had been carved out of bone, and knowing Rieka's fashion sense, they probably were.

Just over her cleavage, the dress was cut in a heart-like shape, teasing a glance at her skin, as if to allure, and entice, before the fabric of the dress clutched her neck-line like a shadowy hand around her neck. The back of the black dress flowed down from the throne, but the front of it was cut higher, stopping just short of her thighs. Or maybe that was just because the skirt of the dress was pushed up to allow the human man to bury his face between her legs.

No wonder Nathaniel was nearly cringing beside me.

Rieka grabbed the hair of the man, yanked him out from between her legs, and elegantly crossed them as she dismissed him with a wave of her hand. He didn't turn to look toward us, just scurried off toward a door behind the throne that I knew from studying the layout of the citadel lead to Rieka's rooms.

Her gold painted lips curved into a smug smile and I forgot all of what Nathaniel had said to me before we entered the throne room because I couldn't just stand there and let her think she had won.

"Right, well, you've seen me now. Can this fucking farce be over now? I'm too tired for this shit."

A muscle ticked in Rieka's jaw, but the smug look didn't fade from her expression.

"Raven." Nathaniel snarled in a chastising tone, and I really wanted to flip him off and tell him to go fuck himself, but I managed to reign in the urge as I kept my eyes on Rieka. I felt a hand brush against my back and could almost hear Adriel's voice in my head telling me that this was a fight for another day, that there were bigger battles to come.

Rieka tapped her nails against the arm of the throne, tilting her head like a viper poised to strike its prey. Her eyes went a brighter shade of yellow as she spoke. "I am truly glad to see that you seem unharmed, Raven."

"I'm sure you've been so concerned for me." I retorted, rolling my eyes.

Rieka's smile curved even more as she sat back, her nails still tapping on the arm of the throne. "I have been. Your disappearance has caused quite a stir within the citadel and afar. There have been acts of rebellion, though those were easily quashed. Attacks on angels outside the citadel increased in the days you were missing and when we were alerted that you had found your way back into the arms of your rebel leaders, I knew where to fetch you from."

A growl rumbled deep inside my chest, and I took a step forward only to be stopped by a firm hand on my shoulder. I glanced at Nathaniel, but he was looking ahead and at his mother. Rieka lifted her right hand and tapped her nails against her chin.

"There can be no uncertainty in the citadel or even throughout the country. I am ruler here. That must be enforced and whilst you were back in the arms of your kind, my rule came under threat."

I opened my mouth to say something smart, Nathaniel's painful squeeze on my shoulder making me clamp my mouth shut. For now.

"I see my son has finally managed to control your smart remarks to some extent. Good. The only reason you are not being staged in the marketplace for all to see and whipped is because Nathaniel bargained with me against it."

Part of me wanted to ask what he had bargained, though I held my tongue as Rieka continued on talking.

"You should know, he did ask that you be left to your people, but that was not possible when the humans were misbehaving. They forged you into a hero, Raven, and heroes don't exist in this world. Therefore, the League had to be sent to haul you back. It paints a clear missive that any who run, any who try and act against me or my rule will be dragged back and made an example of."

Rieka rose from her throne, and I was glad, because it meant that this bullshit was almost over, and I could go wash the dirt off and go and pet Grainger before passing out in bed. Stepping down from her dais, the glint was back in her eyes, and I knew she was about to do something to fuck me over.

"I must assert my rule. Therefore, I will be having a little soiree for angels who are the most influential in the citadel. They must see that I acted swiftly, and you were apprehended and brought back to me. Your presence at the party is mandatory."

I snorted, laughing as I said. "You can fuck right off. I only came back so that you couldn't use my absence as a way to restart a war against the humans. If you think I'm gonna attend a party you are throwing to help you keep the job you're so fucking shite at, you can fuck right off."

Rieka's smile faltered. Her heels clicked against the floor as she strode toward me, looking less like the pampered Imperium and more like the warrior I knew she was. Nathaniel's hand remained clasped on my shoulder, and I had a moment to wonder if he would intervene if she struck me or would just remain rigid by my side.

It wouldn't be the first time that Nathaniel has stood by and watched as his mother tortured me...though, for some reason, now that there was *something* between us, I had to face the fact that if he were to do that now, stand as his mother or Abraxas hurt me, it would shatter something deep inside me.

And this was why I hadn't wanted to make nice with the angels...

Rieka gripped my chin, her nails digging into my flesh. "You will attend. You will attend and you will give the impression that you are compliant and overjoyed to be back in the citadel. You will do this, or I will force you. I will put a collar and a leash on you and drag you on your hands and knees, then make you sit by my feet like the attack dog you are. That will have the same desired effect. It is a choice I am giving you, Raven. Be gracious and accept the easier option."

The Imperium held my gaze for a moment before shoving my face away and turning on her heel to stride from the room without a second glance at me. I stood there, anger bubbling in my veins and pictured her death, Rieka bleeding out from my killing blow.

That image had a smile curving my lips.

T wo days had passed since I had arrived back in the citadel, and it felt like I'd never been away. Having gone back to my room, not saying anything even when Nathaniel told me to get some rest, I went inside and closed the door. Grainger had grunted when I walked in, purring when I rubbed his head, and when he seemed assured that I was okay, he went to sleep and snored his little gargoyle head off.

I'd showered, dressed in comfier clothes, and then slept for ten hours straight, haunted by nightmares. I dreamt of Rieka killing Tiernan and James. I watched as she slaughtered all the Rebels, using Nathaniel's power to incinerate everyone I knew, leaving me alone and powerless. I watched as Rieka realized that she had in fact the biggest bargaining chip at her disposal having learned that the leader of the Rebels was my mother.

The shower I'd had the night before had been wasted when I woke in a cold sweat. I'd showered again, dressed, and headed out of my room to get something to eat. I'd barely made it a foot or two when the door to Verena and Devika's room opened, and Verena had stepped outside.

"I don't need a babysitter." I had growled, still cranky from the nightmares that had prevented any restful sleep.

Verena rolled her eyes. "I'm due to go on patrol in two hours. I'm hungry. You having a babysitter is redundant cause you do what you want anyway."

She took off down the steps and I had to hurry to catch up with her. I reached out and grabbed her arm. "Hey, why are you pissed at me?"

Verena looked at my hand on her arm and I dropped it as she ran a hand through her hair, then sighed, shaking her head. "Fuck, I'm not pissed at you. I've spent the last few days punishing Saskia with her fears and it made me react. I just need not be around you or her for a couple of days and get it out of my system. I'll catch you later."

Verena had walked off then, leaving me standing there. I'd watched Verena go into the room where the League had meals, and went in the opposite direction to the kitchen, making myself some food and taking it back to my room, where I'd stayed until this morning when being in the room had started to grate on my nerves.

I dressed in workout clothes, then headed to the courtyard to release some of the tension. When I pushed open the doors to the outdoor area, I spotted Adriel, who must have had the same idea as me. He seemed lost in his own thoughts as he moved, and I stood there and watched him.

He wielded no blades, just a kendo stick, and went through a serious of movements. His limbs moved like liquid, flowing with ease, each movement an extension of the previous one. The wind howled through the courtyard, the breeze shifting his hair and he turned to face me, bringing the kendo stick sharply against his body to rest.

"I didn't mean to interrupt."

Adriel snapped his wings out and then folded them against his back. "You didn't. I was trying to still my thoughts with meditation, but it did not have the desired effect."

I walked over to where he stood, folded my arms across my chest and smiled. "You wanna beat me up? I'm sure that would cheer lots of people up."

Adriel shook his head, and yet, there was a sliver of a smile tugging at his lips so I would take that as a victory. He strode over and put the kendo stick down before taking a seat on one of the benches. I stayed where I was until he inclined his head for me to take a seat beside him.

Once I had taken a seat beside him, Adriel lifted his face to the sky. "Verena said she snapped at you. The power she wields is sometimes a great burden."

"So is yours, Adriel." I ventured, resting my palms on the bench, and leaning back. "And Verena doesn't have to worry. I've snapped at her enough times. She's allowed an off day, but I will give her some space until she's ready to see me again."

"Nathaniel has been spending time with Saskia to

give Verena a break in case you were wondering why he too has given you space these past few days."

I had been wondering where Nathaniel had been because after acting all possessive and shit, he'd vanished and left me to my own devices since leaving me at my bedroom door. I wasn't gonna go seek him out, mind, because as much as he was being possessive, I really wasn't gonna encourage that. It didn't stop me from asking a pointed question though.

"When you say spending time with Saskia?"

Adriel dragged his gaze away from the sky to give me a look, and I shrugged. I didn't get an answer to my question, though it seemed like Adriel was feeling uncharacteristically chatty this morning.

"It was utter chaos when we realized that you were missing. You were not in any of the places where you tend to frequent and even the humans claimed not to have seen you. It was as if you vanished into thin air."

"I bet you all thought I'd managed to escape."

"Far from it," Adriel told me, turning his head away. "We immediately worried something had happened to you. Nathaniel almost killed Abraxas, thinking he was the one most likely to do you harm. We realized quickly that Abraxas would have made a show of taunting Nathaniel if he had harmed you."

I shivered, knowing that what Adriel had said was the truth. Brax was sadistic enough that he would want an audience or at least want to flaunt his actions to those who cared about me. I think Nathaniel would have killed him if it had been Abraxas and I would have wanted to be around to see that.

"Nathaniel then worried that you might have left because of a disagreement that you had prior to your disappearance. He and Cassiopeia had words, would have come to blows if Makata had not stepped between them."

Damn...

"Once everyone had tempered their emotions, and were able to think logically, we did however come to a consensus as to the most likely fact that you did not escape."

I leaned forward, resting my hands on my knees. "How's that?"

I was looking at Adriel's profile as he said. "I told them that you would not just leave like that. There would have been some signs that you planned to leave. I attested that you would not leave unless forced to do so." His lips curved into a smile. "And while I did not voice my thought, it was Nathaniel who had declared that there was no way that you would leave the citadel with Rieka still alive."

Huh...well... that was very true.

"Saskia chose that moment to arrive back at the citadel. She might have the power to electrocute, and have trained as a warrior, however Saskia never had the mental capacity to be strategic in battle."

I laughed, nudging Adriel with my shoulder. "Is that your very polite way of calling her stupid?"

My question drew a bark of laughter from Adriel. "I suppose so."

"How did you know it was her though? I know she's not the sharpest weapon, but I don't think she flew in and said I dumped Raven in the wastelands."

"She was carrying your axe when she landed beside us. As I said, not very strategic in battle."

Dumb fucking bitch.

"I have never seen Nathaniel so quick to anger as he was in the moment that he realized that Saskia had done something to you. He wrapped his hand around her throat and threatened to fry her alive if she didn't tell him everything that happened and where she had left you."

"He always seems to get angry at me right quick, Adriel. It's not that unusual."

"It was not like that before you. Perhaps it is you that elicits his anger."

I snorted, not really sure I had the right to protest Adriel's claim because as Tiernan would say, I could make a saint mad. My chest ached and I put my palm to my chest and rubbed it.

"You miss the human males."

I nodded, letting out a sigh. "I think this time it's harder, if that makes any sense."

"When you said goodbye at seventeen, you never expected to see them again. It was final."

"Ya, it was easier for me because I thought I'd be dead. But I'd forgotten how much I missed them. The two idiots are my family. Tiernan more or less raised me.

My mam wasn't around too much, and all the memories of me as a child that aren't drenched in blood and war are of Tiernan. And James...there's no one like him."

Adriel chuckled. "He certainly unnerved Makata. I have never seen her so rattled by a male before, human or angel."

A wave of sadness lingered in me, and I didn't know how to quell it, so I sat there in silence with Adriel, missing my brothers but feeling like I had another by my side. I wondered if he would be comforted knowing that I considered him family, never expecting to think of an angel in the same regard.

"You and Tiernan are very alike, yano. Protective. I can see why he looked to you to try and keep me safe. Out of everyone here in this citadel, I'd entrust my life to you."

I remembered then, the massive fucking secret that I was keeping from Adriel. It was on the tip of my tongue to blurt it all out, to tell him that Raisel had not betrayed him, that I had met her, and I think, deep down, she was still in love with him. I wanted to tell him of the strain it must put on her, to be away from him, to have witnessed his torment and stand idly by so as not to blow her cover.

But I couldn't.

I couldn't betray Nathaniel because if I did, there was this part of me that wondered if he would retaliate and put Tiernan in danger, their tentative truce gone up in smoke. Tiernan would not be safe with the Rebels, and he could not be safe with the angels. One way or another, if his secret was exposed, his death would be certain.

And I would have been the one to sign his death warrant.

Gambit.

Rebel.

Traitor.

That was what I had become.

Any words I might have said to Adriel lodged in my throat as he rose, looked toward the door and I snapped my head in the direction of Adriel's gaze. Abraxas stood in the doorway and my stomach immediately plummeted to the ground. A lick of fear crawled along my spine, and I despise that his mere presence had the ability to make me feel weak and afraid.

Abraxas licked his lips, as if he could scent my fear and it excited him. His snow-white wings had grown fully back, and their sheer brilliance of colour was a complete contrast to the rottenness of the angel behind the picturesque appearance. His ice blue eyes held mine, just flickering slightly to Adriel, who appeared as if he was not bothered by Abraxas, though I could tell from his stance that he was ready to defend should Abraxas attempt anything.

"Your commander ordered you to stay away from Raven, Abraxas."

"It seems like she's never alone, Adriel." Abraxas said, taking a step closer. "You and Nathaniel, hanging all over her. Her cunt must taste like ambrosia. Even I want a fucking taste."

He licked his lips then to punctuate his point and I shot to my feet.

"Fuck you, Brax. Your existence is proof that failure has a sense of humour."

Abraxas snarled; his fists clenched by his side. "You can't be protected forever, Raven. If Saskia could get to you then so can I."

I felt a surge of power and glanced over my shoulder to see Adriel's eyes had gone completely black. Inky veins appeared on his face, and I could see them on any bit of skin that was showing. Adriel was the one to lick his lips this time, and his head tilted, like he was sizing Abraxas up.

"Come near me, Adriel and I will block your power."

"Are you so certain that you can?" The coldness in Adriel's tone made me shiver. "The Imperium cannot wield my power as her own. You are a gnat compared to her and you dare think you can command the darkness as your own? This power was not given to me, boy. It was earned through blood and death. I wield it. Me. And you should fear me."

Abraxas looked from me to Adriel, and I wasn't sure if it was out of sheer hubris or stupidity, but he charged at Adriel, looking to clamp his hand on Adriel. I pulled my power to me, lunging for Abraxas, didn't make it in time. The stupid prick gripped Adriel around the throat, squeezed.

Nothing happened.

A chilling laugh escaped Adriel's lips as the black veins crept from Adriel's skin to Abraxas. He tried to pry himself away from Adriel, but whatever power that was contained in Adriel had a taste of Abraxas and wasn't about to let him go. Adriel would kill Abraxas and it would take another piece of the light inside him, the one he'd only recently found.

As much as I wanted Abraxas dead, I wanted Adriel alive more.

Death had latched its teeth into Abraxas and did not want to let go.

I let go of my power, slamming into view as I screamed for someone, anyone to come help. Abraxas was convulsing, his skin pale and almost the same colour as his wings. Adriel looked lost to his power as I heard the flap of wings coming from the sky. I knew they would arrive too late to stop this, to save Adriel.

Grabbing the nearest weapon to me, I swung hard, hitting Adriel in the back and those fathomless black eyes focused on me. A snarl curled his lips, and I tried not to think as I swung again. I didn't see it coming, but somehow, Adriel had knocked the weapon from my hand and had his other hand around my throat.

He lifted me off the ground with a strength that defied possibility. Coldness seeped into my bones, making my teeth chatter and I kicked out, to no avail.

"Please, Adriel." I managed to grind out. "*Please.*"

The coldness left me as suddenly as it had arrived, vicious and painful and it had me sucking in a breath as Adriel let me go, then flung Abraxas at the wall. The asshole angel hit the wall so hard it cracked, and he slid down unconscious. I stumbled backward, almost colliding with Cassiopeia as she looked at Adriel.

"Bloody hell."

Adriel let out a pained roar and then he just dropped, falling to the ground and I rushed over, dropping to my knees in front of his. His chest was rising and falling, which was a good sign, but he was out cold. I watched as the black veins receded, his features returning to normal.

"Hey, come on. Wake up, Adriel."

Nothing.

"Someone get Adair right fucking now."

As if I had willed him to us, Adair landed and stood there for a moment, his eyes wide before I growled at him. "Fucking heal him!"

I felt a hand land on my shoulder, but I didn't care. My focus was on the angel laying on the ground in front of me as his twin dropped to his knees and put a hand to Adriel's chest. Adair flinched and jerked back like he'd been shocked.

"What the hell are you doing?"

Adair shook his. "He's blocking me. How the hell is he blocking me?"

Well fuck this shit...

I grabbed Adriel by his t-shirt and shook him. "Don't do this you stubborn fucking bastard. Let your brother heal you or fucking do it yourself! Stop being a selfish fucking prick!"

Adair braced himself and put his hand on Adriel's chest again. "He's still not letting me heal him but he's not critical anymore. It feels like he turned his power in on himself to stop from hurting you, Raven. It shorted his body out. He just needs to sleep it off."

Relief washed over me, and I sat down, horrified that

there were tears leaking from my eyes. I saw Cassiopeia go to check on Abraxas who was still out cold. I swiped at my eyes as Cassiopeia and Draegan hefted Abraxas off and took him away.

A hand squeezed my shoulder, and I glanced up to see Nathaniel looking down at me. "I'm going to attempt to take him to his room to recover. Hold his hand so he will know I mean him no harm."

"Okay." I reached out and took Adriel's hand in mine, felt a pulse of power and then it was gone. Nathaniel scooped him up carefully and carried him to his recently acquired room. It felt strange being in here like this, but Nathaniel lay Adriel on the bed and stepped back.

Adair came in and proceeded to sit down on the floor beside the bed. I sat down on the edge of the bed, Adriel's hand still clutched in mine. Adriel looked too still, too I dunno, not present and I didn't like it. I didn't like it one bit.

"Raven."

I lifted my eyes to Nathaniel.

"Adriel would not wish to wake and find us here. He will need time to compartmentalize his slip and he would not wish to do it in front of you."

"I can't just leave him." I said to Nathaniel.

"I'll stay with him. I'll let you know when he wakes."

I didn't want to leave him. I didn't. However, I gave his hand one more squeeze and let Nathaniel lead me outside where I turned and told him. "Abraxas went for Adriel. If Adriel isn't alright after this, I'll fucking kill Abraxas myself and you won't be able to stop me."

"Raven."

Shaking my head, I brushed off whatever Nathaniel was gonna say. "No. I let Saskia live. I didn't retaliate when Abraxas tried to rape me. But I will not stand by and let Abraxas be the reason why Adriel retreats back into himself. You hear me?"

Nathaniel's jaw clenched as he nodded. "I hear you."

CHAPTER
TWELVE

T wo days.

Two fucking days and Adriel was still unconscious, and I had spent the most of those two days
pacing and snapping at everyone who came to my door. I
wouldn't listen to anyone who told me that he was okay,
just sleeping off having his power turned in on him, like
a burn out, and only stopped when a fucking exhausted
looking Adair had come to tell me that Adriel would be
fine.

I knew that I wouldn't believe a word until I saw it
with my own two eyes.

On the third day, I couldn't stand to stay holed up in
my room and I went out to the courtyard to burn off
some energy. I wasn't stupid though, and now that both
Abraxas and Saskia were out to get me, I knocked on
Verena's door and told her where I was going, the angel
lifting her brows as if she couldn't believe I was actually

being all responsible and shit and letting her know where I would be.

I may have given her a one finger salute.

Going outside, I stood for a moment, letting the wind chill my skin and I took in some air. I remembered how it had felt coming out here, after being confined to the dungeons for almost three years. I was so consumed with staying alive and finishing my mission that I hadn't taken enough time to soak in the fact that I should have been dead, but instead I was here, heart still beating, even if I was only alive because the Imperium wished it.

It just gave me more time to figure out how to get close enough to try and kill her again.

I had never been one of those soldiers who liked drills and coordinated fighting practice, however, Adriel had shown me that doing the repetitive moves, feeling the weapon as an extension of your person, could make you a better fighter. Walking over to where the kendo sticks were, I picked up two, then positioned myself in the centre of the open space and began to move.

There was no stiffness in my shoulder, no ache in my ribs. Whatever Adriel had done when his power had healed me had taken all the pain away. I lost myself in the routine, mimicking the strikes and movement that I had committed to memory having watched Adriel and dammit if he wasn't right and I felt good, right, balanced.

I snapped my hands in, bringing the kendo sticks to my sternum, exhaling a breath. Sometime during the exercise, my eyes had closed, and my senses seemed to expand because I knew I was no longer alone in the courtyard.

Prying open my eyes, I let my lips curve into a smile as I saw Zephyr standing in the doorway, watching me. He had this cautious expression on his face, and I wasn't sure why. Then it dawned on me that he might be worried that I was mad about what happened the night I came back to the citadel. I mean, I had no real clue how to deal with kids, so I took the easy way out and avoiding doing it altogether.

"Hey Zeph."

"Hi Raven." The young angel said, coming further into the courtyard.

"Haven't you got angel school or something like that?" I asked him, walking over to set the kendo sticks down where they were kept on the rack.

The angel grinned, shrugging his shoulders, his brown and gold wings moving as he did. "I was sent to deliver a message to Devika. I saw you out here and I wanted to watch you."

I laughed, shaking my head. "I mean, that excuse might not fly with your teacher, but I give ya full permission to put the blame on me."

Zephyr gave me a bright smile, and he came forward more. This angel trusted me. I could see it in his eyes. I could ask him to do just about anything and he would do it, because I asked him to. If I was Róisín or Rieka, then I would use his trust as a means to manipulate, to use Zephyr to get information.

"I'm sorry for hurting you." Zephyr said suddenly, dragging me from my thoughts. There was a slight tremble in his tone.

I gestured to my body. "Hey, I'm all good. I was already hurting when you hugged me. It defo wasn't what you did. I just hadn't recovered from having to fight my way out of the wastelands."

His eyes widened, and I cursed inward. Was I not supposed to tell him that?

"That's what everyone was talking about, but I didn't know if it was real or not. My friends, they said that no human could survive the wastelands."

That's because I'm not fully human...

Swallowing back the admission, I also noted that Zephyr had mentioned friends. There were other angelic children in the citadel. I had suspected for a while now, though the fact that Makata was allowing me anywhere near her child had meant that I couldn't probe too much.

"My brothers trained me to fight, and it wasn't my first time in the wastelands. Though those times, I didn't have a dislocated shoulder and hurt ribs."

Zephyr's mouth hung open. "That's so cool."

He was awestruck, believed that I was invincible and that was dangerous for him.

"I almost died. I would have if I hadn't made it home and had my family look after me. One day though, you will be big and strong and a warrior who needs to worry about things like that. Not now though. Just be a kid. That's all you need to be doing now."

I lowered myself onto one of the benches, thinking Zephyr would head off and that would be that, but the angel came over and sat beside me, his wings brushing my side. He turned to look at me, his dark brown eyes warm as he regarded me.

"I didn't know you have a family. Do you miss them?"

I tucked a strand of hair behind my ear. "Ya, I do. My brothers anyways. Me and my mam have a strange relationship. Nothing as good as you have with your mam."

Zephyr smiled. "My mom is pretty awesome. She gets sad though. I think she's lonely."

Nudging Zephyr with my shoulder. "How could she be lonely with an awesome kid like you? And she's got the League too."

"I think she misses my dad. I miss him too, sometimes. I try to remember him, and I listen when mom tells me about him."

Adair had told me that Zephyr's father, Linden, was killed on the other side defending children. The teacher had not been a fighter, but a man who gave his life to defend the defenceless. I also knew that it was Zephyr's aunt who had brought him here, wanting to exploit the warrior he would become in time, and the power he possessed.

"Do you miss your dad?"

I blinked. Choked out a cough and shook my head. Nope, I couldn't miss a bastard who had forced himself on my mam and gave her a permanent reminder of what had happened to her.

"I never knew who my dad was. My mam doesn't talk about him at all. He wasn't like your dad. My dad wasn't a very nice man. But your dad was a hero."

We lapsed into silence then, and I really didn't know what else to say to the kid, so I just went with what I know, and said. "Your power? Does it go both ways? Can you call it to you and send it to someone else?"

Zephyr nodded, then looked around. "I'm not supposed to tell other angels about my power but you're my friend so I can tell you."

I ignored the ache in my chest and pushed to my feet. "Well, since you are already gonna get me in trouble for keeping you from school, you wanna practice your power?"

Zephyr nodded enthusiastically, and we spent a good hour with him summoning weapons and sending them to me. I got used to the shiver of his power in the moment before a weapon appeared in my hand. It felt like an itch I wanted to scratch, giving me the heads up that a weapon was incoming, and then I was able to wield it.

I wanted to test the distance, to see how far Zephyr could project the weapons, so I climbed up to the roof and moved about, getting a laugh from Zephyr as he narrowed his gaze to concentrate. My palms itched and I closed my eyes, reaching blindly for the weapons.

I heard Zephyr whoop and when I opened my eyes, I had two swords in my grasp. Man, I was so fucking jealous of this kid's power. I was about to climb down when Zephyr stretched out his wings and flew up to me, landing on the edge and sitting down.

"That was so cool." He remarked as I sat down beside him, set the swords on the ledge on my other side, watching as he yawned, then rested his head against my side.

"If you fall asleep, you'll fall, and I can't fly to catch you."

"I'm not sleepy. I just want to rest my eyes."

That drew a snort from me, and I just sighed. After a few minutes of silence, I heard boots coming down the hall, watched as Makata ducked her head out into the courtyard, then looked up to where her son was cuddled to my side.

Makata shook her head, but I could see the amusement in her eyes. Zephyr shifted, then shifted closer to me, his head dropping.

"Hi mom."

"When Verena told me that you had vanished from class, having got lost when delivering a message, I was certain you had been eaten by bears."

Zephyr giggled. "Mom, there are no bears in Ireland."

Makata bit back a smile, glanced at me, and I shrugged my shoulders. "We have already established that I am a bad influence so that is the only defence I can offer. Tell V it was all my fault. I distracted him."

I nudged Zephyr. "I can't believe you skipped out on one of Verena's lessons. You'll get me in trouble."

Zephyr looked at me as if he believed me and I laughed so he would realize I was only messing. He yawned again, and I glanced down at Makata. "We did some training, and he used his power a bit so might need a nap. Hell, I need a nap."

Makata smiled, her magenta eyes looking to her son. "Come on, Zeph. Thank Raven and let us go have a snack."

When Zephyr grumbled, Makata tilted her head. "I mean it. If you want to spend more time with Raven, then you need to be able to keep up with her."

That seemed to get through to the young angel, because he hugged me and pushed off the roof, and I jerked, reaching for him when he snapped out his wings and flew to the ground. Right, angel kid, used to throwing himself off rooftops.

Zephyr wrapped his arms around his mam, then waved at Raven before heading inside. Makata inclined her head, made to follow her son and then she paused, as if she was going to say something and I took a wild swing at what it was as I said her name.

"Yes, James is single. Yes, he was flirting with you, and yes, he would put himself in front of any child, angel or human. But I know my brother well enough to know he wants to get naked with you."

Makata rushed off then, and I grinned. James would be a nightmare now when I told him that Makata was attracted to him as well...I mean, if I got the chance to tell him that is.

I wasn't quite ready to head back to my room, and I couldn't bear to go and see Adriel laying there in his bed,

ANGEL'S TRAITOR

so I stayed where I was. Kicking my legs back and forth, I heard the beat of wings and looked up.

Wings of pitch black spanned the sky, and I hated how fucking majestic he looked. Nathaniel flew directly toward me, the storm clouds in his eyes trained on me. His muscular frame was clad in black on black, sculpted to him, a defined delicious body that had me shifting in my seat. Part of me despised that he was fully clothed, hiding all the glory from me, and part of me despised how my body reacted to his mere appearance. His hair shifted in the wind, and his lips curved into a cocky smile, as if he knew I what I was thinking.

Nathaniel hovered down to lower himself to sit on the roof beside me, the feathers of his wings brushing against my spine in an intimate caress that had me shivering, and then glaring at the commander.

His eyes held mine as he said. "Why are you glaring at me?"

"Because you are overstepping." I told him, saw Nathaniel's lips twitch as if he was trying not to smile, or be a smug fucking git.

"You let Zephyr do exactly what I am doing."

I let loose a snort. "Zephyr is a child. I wasn't gonna shove him away cause that can mess with a kid's head or something. And Zeph doesn't have any ulterior motives."

Nathaniel pressed his side to mine, letting his fingers trail over the skin on my arm, making me hold back another shiver. He leaned in, his breath warm on my ear. "And what is my ulterior motive, Raven?"

Rolling my eyes, I shoved him, but he was like a brick

151

fucking wall, unmovable unless you had a shit ton of explosives or a wrecking ball. His wing shifted, moving up and down my spine and I had to supress a groan, trying not to squirm, and let Nathaniel know how much his touch affected me. Though from the smug smile on his face, he already knew.

When I don't answer his question, Nathaniel just chuckles, his fingers playing with the loose strands of my hair. It all too intimate and confusing all at the same time, like we are just two normal people flirting with each other and not the children of two opposing rulers.

"I saw you with Zephyr. I watched you utilize his power."

"I wasn't using him." I snapped, anger in my veins as I went to try and move away from Nathaniel, but his hand landed on my thigh, holding me in place.

"I said utilize, not use, Raven." His palm started to travel up and down my thigh and my brain fogged a little. I swallowed hard, only half listening to Nathaniel as he continued to speak. "I'll get Verena and Dev to expand his training. It never occurred to me that his power might go both ways. You have a brilliant strategic brain that I find very sexy."

Heat flushed my cheeks. My heart is racing, thumping hard inside my chest and I know he can hear it, and I know that he feels the way my body is reacting to his touch. I hate how I've never reacted to anyone in the way I react to him.

Nathaniel settled his hand on the nape of my neck, tilted my head and brushed his lips against my flesh. I clamped my lips shut, hoping to stifle the moan that's managed to claw its way into my throat. His thumb traced my pulse, which was fucking bucking against my skin.

His breath was warm against my ear as he murmured. "Come fly with me."

Sparks ignited inside me. I craved taking to the skies. I needed to feel the clouds with my fingertips. There was a freedom that settled in my bones when I was flying, and I told myself that it had nothing to do with the infuriating angel tempting me.

Shaking my head, I managed to grind out. "No. Actually hell no."

His teeth nipped at my ear, and I yelped in surprise. "Stop that."

"You don't like teeth?" Nathaniel asked me like he was asking me if I liked sweet over spicy foods. He'd use teeth if we ever ended up naked. He'd use them on my flesh, marking me, and he wouldn't be gentle about it.

Why the fuck was that such a turn on?

He nipped again, and I snarled, shoving at him but he still wouldn't budge. Whatever had gotten into Nathaniel today meant that he was done being subtle with his intentions toward me and one of those intentions apparently was to drive me fucking crazy.

"Come fly with me." Nathaniel said again, his tone husky and low.

"Nope. Not interested."

"That's a lie." He chuckled his thumb tracing my jaw.

My breathing hitched and I needed to get away from

him before I let him fuck me on this roof. Just like I'd watched Zephyr do, I shoved off the roof and used my momentum to roll so that when I came close to the ground, I landed feet first.

A dark chuckle sounded above me, and I steeled myself as I looked up at Nathaniel as he mouthed coward. He grabbed the swords, then pushed off the roof to land a couple of yards away from me, putting the swords away before turning to face me.

"Why won't you come fly with me? Give me a straight answer and I'll stop asking."

I weighed up my options and then sighed. "The thrill of flying makes me forget myself. That freedom, it's addictive."

"And it makes you want to kiss me."

I shrugged, folding my arms across my chest. "Don't get ahead of yourself, Nate. I'm sure if Dev flew me somewhere, I'd feel like kissing her too. It's the adrenaline rush, nothing more."

Nathaniel took a step toward me, and I retreated a step.

"Keep lying to yourself, Raven. I can tell from the way your body vibrates when I touch you, when I kiss you. I know you want to do it again."

"Not if you were the last man on earth, Nate, and I was desperate."

Nathaniel's grin can only be described as hungry. "But I like it when you kiss me like I'm the last man in the world. I like having you desperate for me."

I backed away, shaking my head, knowing I was in

trouble, sexy annoying trouble as Nathaniel's laughter followed me through the hall, but the angel himself didn't.

And for fuck sake, I couldn't tell if I was relieved or disappointed that Nathaniel hadn't come after me.

THIRTEEN

Nathaniel had been suspiciously absent from meals and from around me since our heated conversation in the courtyard, and I couldn't help but think he'd done it on purpose, because I can't stop thinking about him and it's really fucking annoying.

The only bit of distraction to come my way was Adair stopping by to tell me that Adriel had woken up. I was walking out the door until Adair put a hand on my arm and shook his head.

"He's not ready to see anyone just yet. Give him space. He will come to you when he's ready."

I wasn't exactly happy about that, but I had bigger things to worry about. The party that Rieka was throwing was in a couple of hours and every bone in my body was urging me not to go. I had this uneasy sensation in the pit of my stomach.

After a workout, I showered and towel dried my hair, leaving it loose in wild curls, then went to my wardrobe and leafed through the sparse clothes I had and realized that I had nothing at all to wear to this bloody thing. Then my lips curved into a smile as I picked out my rebel combats and top, taking my scuffed boots out too. If Rieka was adamant that I attended this shindig, I would rock up as who I was, a rebel, through and through.

A knock sounded on my door, and I called out to come in. Kalila strode in carrying something in her hands, and she gave me a warm smile as she closed the door behind her. Chewing on her bottom lip, the angel looked nervous, her pink and white wings shifting as she moved from one foot to another.

"Hey, what's going on?"

"Please don't be cross with me, Raven." There was a tremble in her voice, like she was genuinely scared of me for some reason, and it didn't sit right with me.

"Kalila, I won't whatever it is, I won't be mad. Come on, we're friends, right?"

Kalila held up the item in her hands. "The Imperium has picked out a dress for you to wear tonight. She has left it to me to ensure that you wear it."

She held up the dress for me to see it fully, and I swear that the moment she twirled it so that I could see it from all angles, I fucking wanted Rieka's blood to coat my hands. The Imperium knew that I wouldn't want to see Kalila punished for my disobedience, that a failure on Kalila's part to force me to do what she wanted, wouldn't sit right with me.

Jaw clenched so tight that my teeth ached, I took the dress from Kalila and looked it over. It was a dress that I would have thought that Saskia would have stashed in her closet, because it left very little to the imagination. The low neckline would give all the angels a glimpse of my cleavage, and short length would barely hit below my thighs. It was made from a material that would cling to my body, not exactly made for fighting in, and it was sleeveless and backless.

My scars.

The dress was designed to show off my scars, to show the angels what Rieka had done to make me her compliant pet. It would be a worse insult to Raven to parade her imperfect skin to the angels than to have her collared and leashed and sat at Rieka's feet.

I shoved the dress at Kalila. "You can go and tell her bitchiness that I'm not doing this. I'm not giving her that satisfaction of walking in there with all my scars on show. She can fuck right off. So, if she wants me there, she can come herself and put her money where her mouth is and drag me on my hands and knees to the party."

"Raven, please. She will only punish you."

I laughed, the sound bitter and twisted. "I can take it. What's another scar to add to the collect, right? Please Kalila, just go. I'm not leaving this room."

The angel wore a crestfallen expression on her face, then set the dress down on my bed before she turned around and walked out the door, closing it with a quiet snick. I sat down on the edge of the bed, scrubbed my hands over my face, and wanted to scream.

I hated all this play of power. I hated it.

A knock sounded on my door, and I snarled. "Kalila, I told you I wasn't fucking going so please, just leave me alone."

The door opened and it was not Kalila who stood in the doorway but Adriel. He didn't look like he was still suffering the after affects of being out cold, but I could see the heaviness in his eyes. He came in and closed the door, then leaned against it.

"I do believe that you are having a negative influence on Kalila."

I snorted. "Why, did she slap you again? Because I really need to teach her how to throw a punch."

Adriel chuckled, shaking his head. "No, she didn't attempt to slap me, although she came to my room and shouted at me so loudly that I had no choice but to come talk some sense into you."

With a sigh, I run my eyes over Adriel. He is dressed in full warrior gear, though it looked more like something you'd wear to ceremonies that to actually fight in. I remember seeing a picture of one of the Rebels in a uniform that he called dress blues, when he was made a garda. That's what it looked like Adriel had on him.

His entire body was clad in black, his bare arms on display. The stitching on the clothes was gold, and he had a dagger strapped to his hip. I had never really seen Adriel carry a weapon before, and it made me curious as to the why he was carrying it now.

He followed where my eyes were, then sighed. "We are given these daggers when we become League. Each of us has one. This is not my original one. I lost mine."

I lifted my gaze to his face, curious to know where he had lost it, and as if he sensed my question, Adriel walked over to the window, gave a snoring Grainger a little pat before he started to talk.

"We were at a party not quite unlike the one that we are about to have to endure tonight. I had been drinking, needing a little extra courage because I was going to ask Raisel to be my mate. I had stressed about it the entire week. We went for a walk outside the citadel and just when I was about to ask her, the Seraphan attacked."

Fuck...I didn't want to hear this. I didn't. Because I didn't want to be the one to mess up and let it slip that Raisel had only been acting on Nathaniel's orders and the woman he loved was behind enemy lines, loyal to her commander and her lover.

"I tried to shield Raisel. I fought hard and my dagger was lost in the fracas. When I knew that I was going to be captured, I turned to tell Raisel that I loved her one last time and she had this blank expression on her face as she shrugged and knocked me out."

"You won't believe me, but I do love him, Adriel."

"I think the idiot still loves you too, for what it's worth."

"It is worth more than you will know."

"Much later, when the darkness had settled inside me, when it had woven its way into my bones, my blood, I killed Aeron to get myself free."

"They had been trying to get information from me for years, forcing me to heal them after skirmishes, and then Khione would chill my blood before Aeron boiled my blood. I could have withstood it all until I heard Raisel's laughter, and

something snapped inside me. I took hold of Aeron's hand and instead of healing him, I stopped his heart from beating. I made his eyes bleed and caused his brain to leak through his ears and nose. I screamed and almost killed everyone in the room. I wanted to kill them all. And now, I can no longer heal."

Adriel rested his hand on the dagger. "Before I got out, before I managed to escape, I went in search of Raisel, and I would have begged her to come with me. However, I underestimated that her love for me might trump her loyalty to Ascian. She stabbed me with her dagger, and I claimed it as my own once Adair had pulled it from my stomach."

I wanted to tell him. I wanted to blurt it all out and tell him that the stupid bitch did love him, that she had never stopped loving him. I wanted to comfort him, but I damn well couldn't and one day, when he found out that I had known all along, Adriel would never trust me again. I would lose him.

"When I came back, I would cover my skin to try and stem the curious and frightened looks from others in the citadel. That was when I ventured from my room. Over time, I stopped caring what others thought of my physical appearance and used their fear to keep them away from me."

Adriel flashed me one of those rare smiles of his then, and I feel like the worst person on the planet. "Then this headstrong girl who carried as much if not more darkness than me demanded that I train her to fight against my own kind. She showed me kindness, acceptance and understanding."

My heart hurts at his words. It hurts so much that I think it might shatter inside my chest.

"Nathaniel, he came to me and told me that by allowing myself to care for someone, for you, it allowed a little sliver of light into the darkness and maybe he was right, light and dark can coexist with one another."

"For so long, my friend, you have held on to the darkness of what was done to you. It consumed you and it thrived inside of you until all you believed was that death was all you had to offer the world. But what you have done this night is proof that there is still light inside of you. It does not have to be one or another, Adriel. There can be both. Light and dark, they can survive in harmony with one another."

Adriel was talking like I was the one who was saving him, and yet, in the end, it might just be my betrayal that sent him plummeting back into the darkness, extinguishing the light that was kindling inside him. Adriel might have survived that kind of betrayal once before... but could it do it again?

He pushed off the door and looked at the dress on the bed. "Wear the dress, Raven. Wear the dress and show them all your scars. Show them just how fucking tough you are. You survived things they could not. Show all the angels who think less of you your strength and let them fear you as much as they fear me."

Adriel opened the door then, telling me he could wait outside and escort me to the party. When he closed the door, I slumped where I sat and reached over for the dress. My refusal to wear it only gave Rieka power over me. I would put on the dress and let the Imperium think she had won this round, but it was me who would claim the victory.

I would use the dress as another piece of armour and a massive fuck you to the Imperium.

I pulled on a pair of underwear and having looked at the dress, realized there was no way I was gonna be able to wear a bra with it, but thankfully, it seemed to have one fashioned into it. I pulled on the dress, shook out my hair and then slipped my feet into my boots.

I mean, Kalia had only brought the dress and like fuck was I going to wear heels.

Not being much of a girl, I didn't know jack shit about make up, so I just pinched my cheeks and put some balm on my lips. I really wanted to wear something to remind them all that I was a rebel, but I didn't even have something of home here with me.

Giving myself a last once over in the mirror, I took a deep breath and after making sure that Grainger was settled, opened the door. When I stepped outside, Adriel was leaning against the opposite wall, his eyes closed, and when he opened them, he blinked in surprise.

"I look stupid." I told him, feeling really self-conscious.

Adriel shook his head. "You don't. I just feel foolish for giving you this whole empowered speech about wearing the dress and showing off your strength when seeing you in that dress makes me want to shove you back inside so that angels won't be looking at you like they want to fuck you."

I can't stop the bark of laughter that tumbled from my lips. Adriel was acting like Tiernan or James might if they were here. He was acting like a brother might to a sister.

"Then you'll just have to stick to me like an octopus because I do not want that sort of attention from anyone. Okay?"

Adriel nodded, then offered me his arm. "Okay."

We walked down the steps and I let Adriel lead me through the halls. Angels and humans alike watched us, some of the angels visibly stepping back out of our way. I tightened my grip on Adriel's arm when I heard the first mummer about the scarring on my back, and Adriel placed a hand over mine.

"Why are they all looking at you all weird?" I asked him quietly, watching another angel take a look at our arms and then back away.

"I do not touch many people. Having you this close to me, shows the other lesser angels that I have some claim to you. That I consider you under my protection. Do not worry, it is different from the way an angel would stake a claim romantically. They know that Nathaniel considers you to be under his protection, but it does not cause any harm for them to know that you are under mine also."

Well, all that is a lot to comprehend and I don't think I have the capacity to really process it right now. It makes me wonder what kind of gestures Nathaniel has made that I'm not aware of to assert that he thinks of me as his...well, not his, but under his protection.

Shit...

I expect Adriel to lead us right to the throne room, but he veered off and steered me into the room where I had slit Saskia's throat. I glanced around, saw that there were other members of the League present. Devika, Makata, Adair, and Draegan were all looking at me with shocked expressions.

"What? What are you staring at?"

They all shared a look, and I looked over my shoulder at Adriel, who just shrugged.

Big fucking help he was.

They were all wearing similar clothes to Adriel, each with their own dagger at their hips. I put my hands on my hips as they looked at each other again.

"Oh, for fuck sake. Spit it out...I already know I look fucking ridiculous."

Devika comes forward, grinning from ear to ear. "No, you really don't. I mean, I know the Imperium was trying to make you look silly in the dress, but I think it's gonna have the opposite effect."

I must have looked confused because Adair offered his opinion. "The dress makes you look desirable. You've been hiding that figure underneath all your usual clothes and now, everyone can see your curves and it will bring you attention."

Devika bumped Adair's shoulder. "What Adair is trying to say is that you look like a woman, and you look hot. Like you should expect a lot of attention."

"I don't want any attention and I certainly don't want to look hot."

Dev grinned, glancing down at my cleavage before shrugging her shoulders. "With breasts like that, I don't think you have a choice. And before anyone wants to make any comments, I can admire Raven's breasts and know that Verena would just laugh. She knows I love her breasts."

Everyone laughed and heat flushed to my cheeks, and I swear my fucking breasts flushed too. Pivoting, I head for the door, but Adriel stepped in front of me. Panic flared in my chest.

"I can't do it. I can't walk out there and have all those eyes on me. I don't want them lusting after me. I don't want that attention. I don't want some sick fuck to rape me. Abraxas, I didn't do anything to encourage him and now he's got a hard on for me."

Reaching for me, Adriel tried to put a hand on me, but I stepped back. "This was a bad idea. A really fucking bad idea."

Adriel stepped closer to me, and I closed my eyes when I felt his hand cup my cheek.

"I would not let any harm come to you. Nor will anyone in this room. If anyone so much as puts a hand on you without your consent, I will make them bleed."

"And me." I heard Devika chime in and then the rest of the League are offering to bloody up anyone who made me feel uncomfortable.

Prying open my eyes, I hold Adriel's dark green eyes, and I notice that they are less dark than usual, shimmering more like his twin's than I think anyone has noticed.

"Besides, we will just let them see you eat some food and once they see you shovelling it into your mouth, your body will lose most of its appeal."

I can't help it, I burst out laughing at Adriel's teasing tone and his eyes lighten another little bit.

Again, I let Adriel take my arm and lead me into the
throne room where the party is in full swing.
Angels and humans mingle together, the lights dimmed,
flames flickering and casting shadows on the walls. I'm
not sure if Rieka has done so to try and create some sort
of ambience, but from the finery that the partygoers
wear, it's easy to see that none of these fuckers are
starving or have ever needed to hunt for their next meal.

My body must have tensed because Adriel looked at
me. I gave him a small smile and exhaled softly. "All the
people starving in this country and there is enough food
in here to feed them for months."

"Back home, we never experienced this. There was no
class division like there is among the humans. If we had
too much food, we shared with neighbours. When we
celebrated, everyone was invited. Zadkiel had fostered
that and while the League were revered as the most elite

of soldiers, the Imperium did not favour opulence like Rieka does."

The others from the League have wandered off, leaving me with Adriel. We wander over to one of the quieter corners and I can feel eyes on us as Adriel pulled out a chair for me to sit. I try and make sure the dress is underneath me as I sit, my eyes scanning the room.

I understand what Adriel meant by opulence. Food and wine are in abundance. The angels and the humans who help Rieka hold the country wear jewels and diamonds that sparkle when the flames of the candles shift toward them. Their clothing is perfectly tailored, looking like something from the history books that I studied growing up.

An angel sits by the stage, playing a harp, and I hate how beautifully she strums the strings, the harp a symbol of Irish history. I don't recognise the song she plays, and when Adriel tracks my gaze to the harpist, he informed me that it was a song from their homeland.

That in itself felt like an insult.

Adriel asked me if I would be fine for a moment while he went to get us a drink, and I nodded, leaning back in my seat as I continued to scan the room. I could feel eyes on me and I wanted to pull my power to me, make myself invisible.

But I couldn't...not when Rieka had yet to grace her own fucking party, knowing she would want to put eyes on me herself to make sure that I had made an appearance. Awareness tugged on my senses, and I shifted slightly in my seat, my eyes landing on Abraxas.

The white-haired angel stared at me; his ice blue eyes fixed on me. Abraxas ran his gaze down my body, and I had to fucking fight my instinct to shield myself from his wandering eyes. He smiled then, and licked his lips, and reached down to place his hand over his crotch.

Bile clawed at my throat looking for release.

"I can't tell if he wants to fuck you or kill ya."

I startled at the sound of a familiar voice as Aoife Lynch sat down beside me. She reached out and tucked a strand of hair behind my ear. "You almost look like a girl."

"What the hell are you doing? They'll suss you for a rebel!" I hissed at Aoife, and she chuckled, running a finger along the slope of my neck and down toward my breasts.

"Relax, Raven. Right now, the angel who has paid for my services tonight thinks I'm trying to persuade you to join us for a threesome. He stupidly thinks that the commander wouldn't kill him for touching you."

My mouth hung open in surprise as I looked over to the angel who was watching me and Aoife. His wings were a mustard kind of colour, his eyes the same and he looked at me and Aoife with lecherous intent. I didn't know how Aoife could play pretend and flirt with creatures who would use her and throw her away if they broke her.

"I know what you're thinking, and I do my part. The elders want me to use my looks to keep me in the inner circle, and I do it. For Meabh. For all the other children yet to be born into this fucked up world. For the children of our generation who didn't get to be kids but had to be soldiers."

I can see the League looking over at me as Aoife placed her hand on my bare leg. Adriel is watching me, waiting for my cue, but I offer him a subtle shake of my head. Instead of pulling back, I lean into Aoife, making it look like I was kissing her cheek.

"How is Meabh?"

I could feel the smile in Aoife's tone. "Running around the place more than usual. Our doctors gave her the once over and it was like she was never sick. You will thank the healer for me since I can't give myself away?"

I nodded then gently reached down and took Aoife's hand off my leg. "I will. Next time you go home, tell the two idiots that I'm okay. But if you tell them I wore a dress, I might just have to hurt you."

Aoife laughed, the sound seductive and not at all meant for me as she winked, gave me one last longing look, then returned to her angel, who gave me a pouty expression like I had ruined all his fun. I watched as Aoife pressed herself against him, then gestured to one of the other couples that were making eyes at them, and they vanished in the crowd.

My job was easy compared to Aoife's. We were both soldiers. I would give my life in order to kill Rieka, and Aoife, she was giving her body to the cause. It was a fucked-up world, and we were all just trying to survive.

Adriel came back over, lowered himself into the seat Aoife had vacated, handed me what looked like wine, lifting his own glass to his lips before he said to me in a low tone. "That is the child's mother?"

I nodded knowing that there was no point in hiding it. I was about to lean forward, then realized doing so would give anyone who looked at me a full on look at my breasts.

"And the child is well? Adair wanted to know."

"She's grand, so Aoife says. She wanted to thank Adair again, but she didn't want to give herself away. Should I be warning her away from the citadel? Will the League out her as a Rebel?"

Adriel took another sip of his drink, then leaned back in his seat, resting one leg over the other. "The woman is fine. No harm will come to her by the League's hand. Others might not even recognise her."

"Thank you."

We sit there for a time, as Adriel pointed out certain angels and humans, letting me know who some of the more influential ones were. I laughed when one of the female angels asked Adriel if he was up for some more intelligent company and he remarked that perhaps he could be if he found someone smarter than the pesky human.

Adriel was fun to hang with at parties.

Time ticked on and still Rieka had yet to make an appearance. Neither had Nathaniel. It wasn't getting late, and I assumed that Rieka would want to make a spectacle when she finally did show up, and to be fair, the less time I had to spend around her was probably better for everyone.

More musicians joined the harpist, including some humans, and the tempo of the music changed from soft mood music to a more alluring sort of tune to get everyone dancing. I tapped my boot against the floor in time with the music, bopping my head, as Adriel watched me with amusement.

"It's not as upbeat as the parties we used to have. Tiernan would get his guitar out and James would use a wooden box to drum out a beat. We would dance and drink and forget the world for a while. Aoife tried to teach me to Irish dance once, then told me that I had the dance moves of a drunk leprechaun."

Adriel scoffed, shaking his head. "Anyone who can fight can dance."

"Well, apparently not me. I'm a much better fighter than dancer."

Adriel was quiet for a moment, then he got to his feet and held out his hand.

"Are we leaving? Please tell me we are leaving."

He shook his head. "Not just yet. Right now, we dance."

"Fuck off," I replied with a snort, thinking he's taking the piss. But Adriel lifted a brow in a silent challenge, and I hated to back down from a challenge.

Slipping my hand into his, I let Adriel draw me into the centre of the dancefloor, as he put his hands on my hips and started to move me in time with the music. There was nothing sexual in his touch, and just as I would in Tiernan and James' arms, I felt safe.

After a few rotations, Adriel let go of my hips and I

moved them of my own accord, feeling like a damn fool as others stepped back to watch us. Adriel leaned in toward me.

"Do not think of it as dancing. Think of it as a fighting stance, of a routine of strikes, like I've tried to instil in you when you do the movements with the kendo sticks. It is only when you think of it as something you are not skilled at, does it make your movements awkward, and clumsy."

Halting my movements, I placed my hands on my hips. "Did you just call me awkward and clumsy?"

Adriel rolled his eyes. "Of course that is what you'd take from my words."

I barely form a smile on my lips when Devika grabbed my hand and starts bouncing around the dance-floor like a hyperactive child. I consider what Adriel told me, then copied Devika's moves, making her laugh and me with her.

The music changed then to something slower as Verena came striding up, winked at me, then pulled Devika to her. They were already kissing when I turned away, my eyes seeking out Adriel, who was now standing off to the side talking to Nathaniel.

As if he could feel my eyes on him, Nathaniel turned his gaze toward me, and I swear that the fire that he wielded with expert ease flared in his eyes. He tossed back the drink he had in his hand, set the empty glass down, and *stalked* toward me.

I felt like prey. I felt like he was prowling toward me, and I had no means of escape.

And from the way everyone had turned to look at the commander of the League of Dominious, they all thought so too. My entire body was on high alert. Everything tightened at the heated look in his eyes and as he continued to devour me with those stormy eyes, I felt like I should run.

He came to a grinding halt just mere inches from me, so close that I could feel the heat of his body along my skin, and it made me shiver. Stubbornly, I lifted my head, letting my eyes clash with his and then he stepped toward me, a hand coming up to clasp my throat.

"Do not worry, it is different from the way an angel would stake a claim romantically. They know that Nathaniel considers you to be under his protection, but it does not cause any harm for them to know that you are under mine also."

His thumb pressed into my jaw as Nathaniel angled my head up so I couldn't look away. His tone is low and husky as he told me. "I argued with mother about forcing you to wear this dress. I never expected to be thanking her."

Rolling my eyes, I let out a sigh. "I look ridiculous."

"Your flesh looks fucking biteable. I want to use my tongue and lips and teeth on it."

Heat flushed throughout my body and Nathaniel's lips curved into a smug smile. "I can work with that."

I don't have the brain capacity to understand his meaning. Then his hands are on my waist, tugging me forward, bringing my body flush against his. The music slipped into another slow melody, as Nathaniel ran his hands up and down my sides, swaying us slightly.

I have no clue what to do with my hands, and Nathaniel seems to sense that, because he puts pause to his caress of my sides, grabs my wrists and forces my hands to his neck. He's taller than me, so I can't quite lock them behind his head, so all I can do is place them on either side of his thick neck.

From the rumble in his chest, Nathaniel approved of where I'd chosen to place my hands. His own hands coming to rest on the curve where my spine and ass were joined, one of his hands stroking up and down and doing nothing to douse the flames that had ignited inside my body.

"Stop trying to cop a feel of my ass, Nate."

Nathaniel lowered his forehead to mine. "You forget I've already had my hands on your ass. I remember the feel of you under my hands. I remember the feel of your body when I made you come. I've fantasised about you coming on my fingers, on my tongue. I've stroked myself to vivid images of you fisting my cock, your hot wet sheath clenching around me."

My cheeks heated, and I tried to duck my head, but Nathaniel gripped my chin. "You make me forget who we are, Raven Cassidy, until I want to claim you as mine in front of every goddamn angel or human in this world."

This feels too intense all of a sudden. I needed to dial it back before we both say or do something neither of us could take back. His lips brush my forehead, and I jerked back, shaking my head. Nathaniel crowded me again, and I put my hands on his chest.

"Listen, Nate," I say with a laugh in my tone. "We

need to take a step back. The dress is not me. I'm not me in this dress. I'm not the type of girl that you would parade about on your arm like Saskia was. It's an illusion, cast by your mother to make me look soft, weak."

"You don't look soft and weak to me, Raven. I can see the strength in your muscles, I can see the power when you move. I know the dress is an illusion but I can't stop thinking about ripping it off you so I can see the real you."

I made to pull my hands from his chest, but he wrapped his fingers around my wrist, holding me in place. I let loose a sigh, closing my eyes for a moment. "C'mon, Nate. Maybe if you went and got laid somewhere else, you wouldn't be fixated on me. I hate this feeling like a show pony. Abraxas has already been leering at me and I've even been invited to a threesome by a human and an angel."

Nathaniel's nostrils flare, his anger now intermingled with his lust. "Which angel invited you to their bed?" His hand is around my throat again. "Everyone in the citadel knows not to touch you. You. Are. Mine."

"I'm not yours, Nathaniel." I answered him softly, patting his chest. "I can never be yours. We both know it. You have to forget this. As much as I might want to let you be mine for a night, we can't lose our heads. You have to let me go."

"You can fuck right off." Nathaniel countered, in an awful accent that I think was meant to sound like mine.

I barked out a laugh at Nathaniel's shite Cork accent and then I just give up. I stepped into Nathaniel's embrace, him releasing my wrists as he realizes I want to wrap my arms around his waist. Resting my head on his chest, I sighed, then felt his arms come around me, and Nathaniel said nothing else.

The music continued for what seemed like forever, then suddenly it cut out. A commotion started around us and I lifted my head from Nathaniel's chest. Turning away from him, I feel his hands on my waist as the crowd parts and I know now why the entire party had come to a halt.

I might hate Rieka, but there is no denying that she knows how to make an entrance. She commands the room. Her hair is braided into an elaborate twist that is both delicate and fierce at the same time. Instead of her usual outfits that show off her muscles, her strength, tonight the Imperium had decided to go for a more restrained look.

The dress is high necked, a mixture of what looks like satin and lace, the lacework on the bodice and skirt almost resembling Celtic knotwork. The lace is almost gunmetal in colour, shimmering against the black. Her arms are covered, but the dress does not take away from how voluptuous Rieka is. The waist of the dress is cinched in so tight that it must not be comfortable.

Rieka was a lethal beauty, breathtaking to look at but under the surface, inside her core, she was ruthless and cold. She had everyone's attention, and she loved every minute of it.

Her wings are held tight against her back as Rieka strode forward, her chin in the air. I felt Nathaniel's hands grip my hips tighter, as if he was afraid that I would step into Rieka's trajectory, but Nathaniel didn't need to be worried about any of that. As she moved, Rieka's yellow eyes scanned the room, searching, seeking, and I know she is looking for me.

When her eyes finally landed on me, the Imperium's lips curved into a sinister smile.

And it chilled me right down to the fucking bone.

R ieka comes toward me, the skirt of her dress swishing against the floor. Everyone is watching us now, waiting to see what the Imperium would say to the human, and what the Imperium would make of the possessive hold that her son has on my hips. His fingers are digging into my hips, hard enough to bruise, but I don't dare tell Nathaniel to loosen his grasp.

She came to a stop in front of me, the gap between us almost non-existent, and my palms itched for a weapon, hell even a fucking fork to pierce it right through her yellow fucking eyes.

That would make the angels fear me.

Rieka's eyes scanned down my person slowly before coming all the way back up to my face. She tilted her head, that smile still curving her lips as she regarded me. "Raven."

All she said was my name, so I addressed her right on back. "Rieka."

The angels around me gasped in shock, and Nathaniel's grip changed. One hand slid up to cup the nape of my neck and he gave a slight squeeze in warning, like he was telling me to be careful. A nervous chatter had started around us, cutting off completely when Rieka held up her hand. That hand then reached out and gripped my chin, her nails, sharpened like a blade digging into my flesh.

Nathaniel's grip on my neck eased as Rieka shifted my neck from side to side, and I knew he had done it so as not to hurt me. Rieka's other hand trailed down my arm, then back up, resting on the front of my chest. She tapped her nails against my skin, her smile deepening.

"I must say, dearest Raven, that all dressed up like so, you almost look like a civilized person and not a filthy Rebel."

Letting loose a snort, I wave a hand between us. "I must say, dearest Rieka, that all dressed up like so, you almost look like a leader and not just a cold-hearted murderous bitch."

There is an outcry around us, as we lock gazes, neither of us willing to back down. Rieka removed her hand from my face, tapping her nails perilously close to my heart before she took a step back. If this whole party was for Rieka to assert her dominance over the angels, show them that I had been recaptured and she had put me back in my place, then why the fuck was she not striking me and making an example of me?

Rieka lifted her gaze to her son, studied his body position and I could tell she was looking to where

Nathaniel was cupping the nape of my neck. She tilted her head to the other side. "Have you considered my offer?"

"I told you there was nothing to consider."

"As you say." Rieka responded in a bored tone, and now I wanted to know what the fuck Rieka had offered him.

The Imperium strode away from us then, and I watched as Cassiopeia walked after Rieka, her royal blue eyes landing on me and Nathaniel, before she went to stand beside Rieka on her dais. The music started up again and Nathaniel released my neck.

Turning to face him, his expression was grim as I arched a brow. "You wanna tell me what that was about?"

"A power play by mother." He ground out, grabbing my hand, and stalking over to where the rest of the League, minus Abraxas and Saskia, were as Nathaniel hoisted himself up on once of the perches and yanked me toward him.

Setting my hands down on his thighs so he couldn't pull me flush against him, I lifted my brows. "I bloody know that Nate. But what did she mean by", I aim for my best snotty bitch voice and echo Rieka's words, "Have you considered my offer?"

I heard a teeter of laughter, though it's quickly halted when Nathaniel runs a hand through his hair. "It is nothing that concerns you. I have said no. That will be the end of it."

"Yeah, right." I heard Adair mumble under his breath,

then the healer flushed, looking at his wine glass before setting it down.

I gave Nathaniel a shrug, then stepped back. "I'll find out eventually. You know Rieka, if it involves me, then she will get all riled up with glee to tell me. You have two choices, bird boy. You tell me what's going on, or I walk right on up to mommy dearest and ask her myself."

Nathaniel doesn't respond as quickly as I would have wanted him to, so I spin around, about to make a beeline for the Imperium when I feel a hand rest on my shoulder. But it's Adriel who has halted me, not Nathaniel.

"Don't."

That was all the Adriel said, and I listened to him, knowing it must be fucking awful for Adriel to step in between the newest installment of the Raven and Nathaniel drama fest. Clamping my mouth shut, I turned back to Nathaniel and arched a brow. I wasn't going to let this go. I needed to be clued in with all the facts in order to best prepare myself for whatever Rieka had in store for me.

"When we returned to the citadel, the Imperium made me an offer. Take a mate chosen by her to stand beside me when my time comes to be Imperium, and she would let me keep you, as a mistress. I could be with you once an heir had been conceived."

I'm silent for an entire minute before I started to laugh. Whatever Rieka had said, there was no way she would let me live once Nathaniel had done what she asked him. The moment an heir was conceived, I'd be dead. And that was even before you took into consideration that Rieka thought I would be amenable to accepting a role as Nathaniel's bit on the side.

"She knows that you'd never fuck that stupid sparkly bitch ever again, right?"

Nathaniel lifted his gaze to mine. "It was not Saskia that she offered to me."

Dragging my gaze from Nathaniel's, I glanced toward the dais to see Cassiopeia watching us, her eyes flickering to Nathaniel before shifting back to mine. I saw how much she despised me then, though I couldn't be certain if it was because I was human, or because Nathaniel had a thing for me.

Nathaniel refusing to take her as a mate or whatever must have pissed her off.

I think back to the heated conversation that me and Cassiopeia had before Saskia kidnapped me, how I accused her of being jealous of me and Nathaniel. Had Cassiopeia gone to Rieka to suggest becoming Nathaniel's mate to get one over on me? Or was she actually in love with Nathaniel?

I might not have wanted Nathaniel to end up with Saskia, but as much as I hated to admit it, Cassiopeia would be the kind of mate he could have by his side. She was a warrior, her power was terrifying, and most importantly, she was an angel.

Jealously raged inside me and I let loose a growl, stalking away from the member of the League and went in search of a drink. I waited until one of the humans had taken a drink from one of the glass decanters, then poured myself one and knocked it back.

"Miss Cassidy?"

Setting my glass down, I turned to see a human male standing in front of me. He was slightly taller than me, with dark brown hair that was receding. He had a rounded belly, no doubt one of the Imperium's influential humans who she kept around to give the impression of cooperation, but there was no doubt this pitiful excuse of a man was a tool for Rieka to use.

I just stared at him, not bothering to respond and this man gave me an amused smile. "I can see your mother in you. She once looked at me with the murderous intent that you have in your eyes."

My heart skipped a beat. He better not spill to the Imperium that my mother was now the leader of the Rebels and get me fucking killed. I arched a brow as if to warn him and he chortled, shaking his head.

"I have not said a word about that. You have my word."

"Sure," I remarked with a snort. "I don't know you from Adam and you expect me to believe that you haven't offered up to the Imperium that juicy nugget of information? Do I look that gullible?"

"My son was taken by the Seraphan. I have not seen him in five years. I work with the Imperium to try and get information on his whereabouts."

"I hate to tell ya, Rieka doesn't give a flying fuck about your son, and she would walk over his dying body if it meant getting something she wanted. You want to find out about your son, then talk to the commander."

The man shifted looking from me to Nathaniel, then

back at me again. "I came to speak to you because everyone knows within the citadel, you curry the commander's favour. If you asked him about news of captives from the Seraphan, then he would tell you. I would reward you kindly for the information."

Now it's my turn to laugh, shaking my head. "Yano, if you'd come and made this offer while I was rotting in the dungeons right below our goddamn feet, then maybe I would have done something. And yet, why does your son matter more than the hundreds of men, women, and children who have disappeared at the hands of angels."

The man swallowed hard, and I think he would have walked away; however, I wasn't done yet. I pointed to the space just before the Imperium. "I snapped the neck of a human who killed an angel for raping and discarding her brother's body in the wastelands. Her name was Noelle, and she was a farmer, not a fighter. I killed her as a mercy. So, if I ever come across a man who looks overfed and pompous enough that he might be your son, I'll kill him quick and painless. He doesn't deserve anything else."

His mouth hung open and I made to walk away, but the stupid prick grabbed my arm and called me a bitch. I gave him one chance to remove his hand from my arm, and when he didn't, I ducked under his arm, swept my boot out to knock him off balance. He landed on the floor with a bang that echoed throughout the room, and then I put my boot on his chest and looked down at him.

"I'll tell her who you are. I will."

I pressed my boot down harder on his chest, probably giving him an eyeful up my dress as I did. "Not really the best incentive to keep you alive there, buddy, is it?"

"Raven."

I ignored the command in Nathaniel's tone, my eyes focused on the worm beneath my boot. "Not your fight, Nate. Not your fucking fight."

"I was merely going to say that if you want to dispose of him, then killing him here is not the best place. Too much white that will make the blood difficult to get out."

That made my lips curve into a smile as the human paled even more. "You do say the most romantic things to me, Nate. Give me a blade and I'll try and make as little mess as possible."

Hands clapped from the dais, and I shifted my gaze to where Rieka lounged on her throne. The crowd of angels and humans parted, and I could see clearly as Rieka got to her feet, watching me but I wasn't going to budge even if she asked me to.

My hair moved across my shoulders, as Nathaniel gripped the back of my neck again. He didn't say anything, his body vibrating behind mine, so I removed my booted foot, and let the weasel scurry back and disappear into the throng of people.

"Nathaniel, bring your human pet closer."

A snarl escaped my lips as Nathaniel sighed, then strode forward, giving me no choice but to let him. Adriel fell into step beside us, and I could sense the rest of the League inching closer, as if they too could sense that Rieka was finally about to reveal whatever the real reason for this party was and what she had cultivated in her twisted mind as a way to put me back in my place.

"As amusing as that little display was, it is time for a far more interesting piece of entertainment." Rieka's eyes were solely focused on me as she fanned out her dress and then began to walk back and forth across the dais.

"Everyone gathered here today, is well aware of the rebel scourge who continue to defy my reign and fight a battle that they will never win."

I snorted, wishing I could flip her off, but I can feel Nathaniel tense as a board behind me, and a brush of fingers told me Adriel is by my side. No one dared to say a word as they gave the Imperium their full attention, and she continued her speech to her rapt audience.

"I allow their existence because it amuses me. I could at any moment, give my son an order to fly down to their base and eviscerate every man, woman, and future rebel, with his fire. I choose not to do that. I choose to let them live."

I see the way that she skirted around the whole men, women, and children part. There are a lot of monsters in this room, me included, and even they would be appalled at harming an innocent child. I think of Meabh and Zephyr, two children who may be at war with one another in time, and all because this bitch ordered it.

"Saskia, a member of my League, felt the threat of a human inside the walls of the citadel and acted out of the interest for her Imperium and her fellow angels. She has faced consequences for her actions, a deviation from her orders, though well meaning, and will face no further punishment for her actions."

Well, the whiff of bullshit coming from the statement was evident.

Rieka must have seen my expression, because she stopped, stared down at me, clasping her hands in front of her. "Raven, you have proven yourself to be both an asset and a troublesome pet to have within the walls of my citadel."

"That's the nicest thing you've ever said to me, Rieka. Maybe we could bond over a girl's night. Braid each other's hair. Talk about boys."

Adriel let out a startled laugh, and when Rieka's eyes shifted to glare at him, Adriel glared right on back, and it was Rieka who drew her eyes away first, bringing them back to me.

Rieka flashed me a smile that was full of teeth. "You have a disregard for authority that has me wondering if your own kin sent you to kill me because they wanted rid of you."

"I'm the gift that keeps on giving. They sent me to you and I won't get sent back until you are dead or I am."

"Sometimes, Raven, death is the easy way out. Or have you forgotten how you once begged for death when Abraxas whipped you?"

My skin tingled from the weight of eyes on my back, eyes on my scars, and I jerked my chin up to show Rieka I didn't care about my scars, or what was done to me. I was still alive; I was still here. I was still defying her.

"You and your Rebels are insignificant. Easily felled.

You are insignificant. That is something that you need to realise and accept. This defiance that I allow, it only forces my hand to make sure that I pull you back in line. I could order you back to the dungeons, put you in an even darker hole, and chain you up so that you are unable to protect yourself."

I held my ground, not so much as blinking.

"Grant them no mercy."

I heard my mother's voice in my head and stiffened my spine.

"Perhaps I would let someone bring you snippets of information. How a band of angels took out one of those rebel holes they think we don't know about? Maybe I'll come by myself and rattle off names to see if you recognise someone that means something to you."

I had always known the Imperium was a cruel heartless, bitch, and now I could add vindictive to that list. But in making this all about me, about punishing me, Rieka had made one fatal mistake...she had played her hand and revealed that I had gotten under her skin, that I was in her head as much as she was in mine.

"Angels will always have more power over humans and not just because we have powers. We are a superior race. Stronger. Faster. A species as close to perfect as one can get, and the humans need to accept that and bow down before us."

Rieka waved a hand in the air, that sinister smile returning. "But as much as this event was to prove to the naysayers that I had the power to recapture the rebel who once tried to murder me, and I still am magnanimous enough to grant her a stay of execution, the Rebels must learn that I am not to be trifled with."

Nathaniel's hand finds its way to my hip, and I pull my gaze from Rieka's to try and get a glimpse of his expression, but his features are an unreadable mask.

"The humans I so graciously allow to stay within my citadel, giving them stability, a purpose, are mine to do with as I please. With that said, it is time for the entertainment for the evening. I thought that it had been a long time since we had a good auction. I do hope everyone is in the buying mood."

I take one look at Rieka's smug face and then my gaze snapped toward the door that Abraxas opened, and even before anyone stepped through it, I knew, I just knew that this was gonna be bad.

The humans shuffled out one by one, and my first instinct was to try and help them. I took a step toward the dais, only to be stopped by Nathaniel's arm around my waist, preventing me from surging forward. I'm forced to watch as one by one, the humans file out of the door, then they stop as the chain around their waists is halted by whoever is giving Abraxas shit and not wanting to come out.

I watched as Abraxas snarls, slipping inside the doorway and forcing a figure to stumble out, landing on his knees and I sucked in a gulp of air. My heart started to race as the man's blond head, with hair caked in blood, lifted, and instantly eyes collided with mine.

His face was battered and bruised, his lip split, and he had ligature marks around his neck. But I'm power-less to do fucking anything as Abraxas drags him from the ground and shoves Hayes forward, and the rest of the chained humans amble to the top of the dais.

A few of the humans have blank expressions on their faces, one of the younger looking boys is crying, and I try to school my expression, so Rieka doesn't realize that Hayes means a lot to me, even if he is an asshole.

"Hold, Raven. Hold." Nathaniel mumbles to me, but I can't just stand here while that bitch sells one of my closest friends off like he's fucking cattle. No matter what had happened between us in the past.

Abraxas came forward and unlocked the chains from around their waists, but their hands were still cuffed together. I ran over all the possibilities in my mind, all the ways in which I could put a stop to this, and yet, on some level I already knew that Nathaniel wouldn't let me.

Some of the angels and humans are taking the opportunity to leave, and I catch sight of Aoife slipping out unnoticed, though she spots me watching her, puts a hand to her chest, and then she's gone, away from all this mess and I let out a sigh of relief.

"These humans have defied the rules I have set out for them, the rules that allow them to remain within the walls of my citadel. Therefore, those freedoms have been revoked and they require new masters to ensure that they understand that rules are not for breaking."

Rieka strutted down the line, walking right down to where Hayes was standing, and my stomach dropped before she walked back to the top of the line. Rieka put a hand on the young girl's shoulder, and the girl shuddered, her lips trembling as if she was about to burst into tears.

Don't cry. Don't give them any of your tears...I pleaded with her in my head.

"This girl was working for the kitchen washing dishes and she was caught stealing more food than was allocated to her. The girl is untainted. Her virtue is still intact. She is available to any angel with a good enough offer."

I'm sickened as the angel who wanted me to join him, and Aoife stepped forward and licked his lips, offering Rieka enough gold coin to fill my bedroom. Rieka accepted his offer, had Abraxas unlock the girl's hands, and when she is dragged past me by the angel, her eyes are dead.

One by one, Rieka moved down the line, listing out their supposed crimes, and offering them up like their lives mean fuck all to her. They don't, I know. That's her entire point. Human lives are nothing but currency to Rieka and I have never wanted to kill her more with my bare hands than I do in that moment.

I have to focus now, because she's getting closer and closer to Hayes, and the stupid fool is looking at me, at Nathaniel's arm around my waist, and I can tell he is furious. That idiot is more worried about what I am doing with the commander than what is about to happen to him.

"Do not let Hayes go back to the citadel. It will get him killed. He will get himself killed."

I'd called it. I'd told them not to let him come back. This anger he had for Nathaniel. This rage he had because he saw me as his and didn't like the fact that I had told him that being near Nathaniel set my fucking soul on fire, was consuming him.

Rieka put both hands on the last remaining woman and squeezed her shoulders so tightly I saw the girl wince in pain. She tried to shift, but Rieka just dug her nails into the woman's flesh, making her bleed. "This human thought that a pregnancy would raise her above her station. She had a nice home with an angel of high class, and she tried to trap him with a pregnancy that goes against every law we hold most dear."

I'm frozen. I'm the stillest I have ever been, and I know that Nathaniel can hear the rapid racing of my heart. Does Rieka know what I am? Is this all for me? If she knows what I am, then why the fuck is she not using it to her advantage? If the angels in this room knew that part of me was angelic in nature, it would cause an uproar.

"The abomination has been terminated, and her angel has dispatched her from his household." Rieka turned to look at an angel who looked brutally cruel, her wings a bright orange, with tan features sprinkles throughout. Her lips curved in glee at the sight of the pretty young woman.

"Jophiel, I assume that you can made use of her at one of your ventures?"

The other angel inclined her head. "I'm sure she will be a popular attraction, Imperium. She would be broken in within the week, would know her place then."

Fuck, they were sending the girl to an angelic brothel.

"Then she is a gift to you, for the worthy service you provide."

This bitch, this Jophiel, inclined her head again. "You are kind and generous with your gifts, Imperium."

Rieka shoved the young girl toward Jophiel, and she shuddered, as Jophiel smirked. "I do hope you have strong knees, girl, because you will spend quite some time on them."

"She has a high pain threshold. Abraxas can confirm that."

My head snapped toward Abraxas, and I snarled at the way he licked his lips and mouthed *you're next* to me. Jophiel led the girl away, and then there were only two men left, one of them being Hayes.

Rieka focused on the man standing next to Hayes, and it's then I recall that this is the man who I had seen between Rieka's legs when I returned to the citadel. Rieka walked around to the side of him, then gripped his chin, jerking his head up.

"While there is no denying that this man has been a gracious lover that has kept me entertained the past few weeks, I'm afraid he was only too eager to spill human secrets to me. If he was so willing to sell out his own people, then he would have no qualms of doing the same to angels. I believe he had used his position to hold on to the information and was ready to tell the Rebels of the location of our most vulnerable."

I lost all sympathy for the fucking idiot when I heard that.

Rieka lifted her gaze to me, and I swallowed hard.

What the hell had this man found out that would have her do this in public.

"He was only too eager to inform me of all the times that you have been seen down in the human servant quarters. That you may have been spilling angelic secrets to the Rebels who think I do not know linger in my citadel."

Molly needed to get every single human out of the citadel. Rieka would weed them all out and kill them all, just to spite me and give her something to do for an afternoon.

"And I was quite interested to hear that while you have been a thorn in my side having captured my son's affections, you have also been hiding your lover among the humans and cavorting with him right under my son's nose."

Nathaniel's arm around my waist pinned me too him, but I saw him snap his gaze toward Hayes. I had told him about sleeping with Hayes but hadn't told him the name. Both Dev and V were looking from me to Hayes, because they too recognised him as the boy they had brought to my room.

I had to deflect attention from Hayes. I had to make them all think that I didn't give a fuck about him.

I let loose a bark of laughter, shaking my head, pleading with Hayes in my head for him to understand. Elbowing Nathaniel in the side, I stepped free of his grasp. I kept laughing, then doubled over as if what Rieka was saying was the funniest thing in the world.

"Him? You think I've been sneaking off to have secret

sexcapades with him? Come on, Rieka. I don't care about him. Not in the slightest. That is the dumbest thing that you have ever said to me, and you've said a lot of dumb shit. Oh my god, that's fucking hilarious."

The laughter died in my throat when Rieka swiftly snapped the neck of her former fuckbuddy, leaving Hayes as her only victim on the dais. If I went invisible now, would Nathaniel even try and stop me from saving Hayes? Or would he restrain me, and force me to watch as his mother killed my friend.

"She's telling the truth."

My head snapped up to hold Hayes gaze, as he licked his lips, and then glanced at the Imperium. "She doesn't care about me. Not in any way that matters. Hurting me to get to her won't work. It's a waste of your time."

Rieka grabbed Hayes by his hair and licked up the column of his neck. My fists clenched by my side, but I made no move to stop her.

"Perhaps I should give him to Jophiel also. He is unique looking enough to make some decent coin, since you don't care about him, not in the slightest." Rieka leaned in again but this time, she kissed Hayes, and my knees almost gave out.

"He tastes like rebel scum..." Rieka said with a snarl when she broke the kiss, her nails digging into his chin, and I saw the trickle of blood dripping down. "Don't you, Michael?" Rieka smirked as she looked me dead in the eyes. "Or should I call you Hayes now that we are well acquainted?"

This was bad...this was very fucking bad.

"Childhood friends, are you not? It would make sense as you are both similar in age and that accent is unmistakable. You thought you could hide from me, work an angle, and try and follow through on a plan to poison my son?"

Oh Hayes. You stupid fucking prick. Sloppy. You should never have been a soldier...this war was something you were not built for. And now, it would be your undoing.

I tried to hold on to my training, on to the part of my brain that could compartmentalize what was gonna happen, and yet, I took an involuntary step forward, and this time, it was Adriel who gently rested his hand on my elbow. From the expression on Rieka's face, she knows she has won this round, that she could ask me to do anything, and I would do it, to keep that stupid prick safe.

Hayes bowed his head, and his shoulders slumped. Fight, you fucking idiot, fucking fight...that's what I want to scream at him. I want to storm up on that dais and shake some sense into him.

"Makata, come here a moment."

I blinked, turning my attention back to Rieka, as the angel with the powers to change shape glanced at Nathaniel and me before going to stand behind Hayes. I'm not entirely sure what Rieka's intentions are, but I know it's nothing good. Rieka made a show of lifting her left hand in the air and letting it settle on Makata's shoulder, and I could feel the ripple of her power from where I stood.

Makata is looking at me, her magenta eyes full to the brim with sorrow and tears sting the back of my eyes. I'm forced to watch as Rieka's other hand morphed into wicked claws and my blood ran cold inside my veins.

Hayes lifted his head and gave me a sad smile. Then he said out loud for everyone to hear. "It's okay. I love you. It's okay."

I want to be someone else, someone who can lie and tell him that I love him too, just not in the way he wanted me to. That he was my brother, my friend, and I will never forget him. I can't. I can't get the goddamn words out and then Rieka's clawed hand swiped across Hayes' throat.

I screamed, I couldn't stop it from escaping my mouth as Hayes clutched at his throat, the blood gushing from the wound, and then he's falling to the floor. I know he's dead, because his hands fall away from his throat, his eyes staring at me, the last thing he saw before his world went black. I want to scream for Adair to heal him, to bring him back but I can't, I won't. Even Adair couldn't save the dead.

Rieka removed her hand from Makata's shoulder, then held her hand out and Abraxas gave the Imperium a cloth to wipe Hayes blood from her hands. "I always win, Raven. In the end, I always win."

I'm unmoored, lost in a sea of grief and regret and I can't think of a snappy comeback to throw at her, to get the last word in like I always try and do. There was nothing I could do to save him. Nothing.

"You look at him like you've never looked at me. He

touches you and you give him this look that I've never seen before. How can you let him touch you when, after all we've been through, you flinch when I look at you. You have to know that I'm in love with you, Raven."

My heart continues to beat painfully.

"It's okay. I love you. It's okay."

Another beat, another breath as someone said my name.

"She doesn't care about me. Not in any way that matters. Hurting me to get to her won't work. It's a waste of your time."

He died knowing I didn't love him, thinking I didn't care about him.

"You have to know that I'm in love with you, Raven."

I had used him and discarded him, and my actions brought us here, not Hayes'.

"You have to know that I'm in love with you, Raven."

It was my fault...all my fucking fault.

"It's okay. I love you. It's okay."

Rieka is studying me, glee in her yellow eyes and then she motioned with her hand to Abraxas. "Bring in the next ones."

I look at the doorway as Abraxas stalked through and then two teenagers came out that I recognised from Molly's kitchen, and then I heard a voice swearing, and Abraxas, he all but carried a woman out over his shoulder.

He set the woman down on her feet, and she spat in Abraxas' face. His palm slapped her so hard across the face that she stumbled, landing in the blood beside Hayes' dead body, and then she looked up at me.

Aoife.

Abraxas had slapped Aoife and Rieka was going to kill her. Fear and adrenaline light a fuse inside my veins, my heart beating way too fast, my vison was blurred and I'm struggling to breathe.

It feels like I'm having a panic attack. It feels like I am losing my shit and if I do lose my shit, then Aoife was gonna die, and Meabh, who Adair saved only days ago will grow up without her mam. She would become another orphan child and I couldn't let that happen.

I couldn't.

My power is shimmering inside of me, whispering at me to let go of control, to let go of all the pain. I gave Aoife a small nod, as I simply stop holding back my power. It raged, rushing over me like a wave, and it built, and built until it burst from me and pain like I've never felt ravaged my body.

Rieka is shouting for someone to secure the humans and I know I've used my power to shield them from angelic view. I heard myself shout at Aoife to run, focusing my power on them, until Aoife scrambled to her feet, grabbed the two men and then she's fleeing, and I could feel her moving further and further away from this room and the citadel.

The power inside me lashed out, snapping back at me and I screamed again, the sound not entirely human. Blood trickled from my nose, as Nathaniel tried to get through whatever barrier my power has erected around me, but it won't let him through.

"Nathaniel, kill her."

"No. I will not."

"You defy me? For her?" I heard Rieka say sounding utterly taken aback.

"Yes, for her, I would."

My body started to tremble, and my teeth clacked together. I tried to put a leash back on my power, but it had had a taste of unrestrained freedom and it wanted more. Something inside me told me that I hadn't even begun to test the extent of my power, and I could do more, be more than I ever imagined.

I was drunk on the power.

"Raven, pull it back. Pull your power back. The humans are safe."

Adriel's voice reached me, and I coughed, a coppery taste in my mouth, as I dropped to one knee, vomited blood on the ground, and placed my hands to my ears and screamed as pain seared through my entire body.

"She's killing herself! Her entire body is haemorrhaging, I can feel it. Someone bloody help her."

I laughed at the sound of Adair's concern, the sound coming out as a gargle as blood filled my field of vision, and my other leg gave out. My power snapped back to me so suddenly, I convulsed, the last thing I'm aware of is Nathaniel lunging for me.

Then there is nothing but oblivion.

SEVENTEEN

I stood on the edge of the cliffside, the roar of the wind and the crashing of the waves like a symphony. The gusts slammed into me, trying to knock me off balance, however I stood firm as I looked out at the Irish sea. The waves seemed angry today, enraged as they smashed into the cliff, spraying me with droplets of water. The clouds mingled in with the shadows, creating a skyline of grey and white, the roll of the waves making it look something that would have been printed on a postcard, back when the world was a different place.

Closing my eyes, I inhaled, then exhaled, letting this little sliver of peace wash over me. Standing here, in the open space of lush green and ocean blue, I could almost forget the pain that echoed throughout the land, the death, the war, the devolution of society. I could ignore the scars on my skin, the battle wounds etched there, woven like tattoos into my flesh.

It didn't matter who or what I was standing here on this cliffside.

I was insignificant to the landscape, and I found I liked it that way.

I felt weightless here, unburdened, and that was why I continued to come here, to gaze out at the sea and wonder where I might end up if I was free to travel across the sea, through the shadows and to the world beyond. No one knew if the world had continued since the start of the new world, or if Ireland had simply vanished covered by shadows.

I used to wonder would the other countries try and send some sort of sign that they were out there, ready to offer aid? But my mother told me that I was being ridiculous, that the shadows that surrounded Ireland had most likely sniffed out any life around the world and we humans were the last remaining hope of mankind surviving.

And then she would look at me, and her expression would tell me all I needed to know about how she felt about me, because she didn't see me as human. I was never a person to her. I was simply a constant reminder of what was done to her, what creatures had done to her and her people.

The waves hit the side of the cliff and I opened my eyes. I wasn't going to let the horrid things my mother said to me once ruin this feeling. She was long gone and yet, her voice still haunted me, as did the voices of those I had once called family.

It seemed a horrible twist of fate that while I remained youthful, as immortal as the angelic side of my DNA, those I loved had withered and died as I watched on. There was no one left now that remembered the rebel I once was.

To them I was always going to be part monster.

I was exposed on the cliffside, open to attack, but it was rare I was allowed the space to have some time to myself. The Imperium did not like to leave me out of his sight for too long, because it was well established that I was a magnet for trouble.

But he knew that the Commander of the League of Dominious was never too far from me...

He too, had difficulty letting me out of his sight.

Glancing up at the disappearing day, I knew this little piece of solace was disappearing, and I would have to return to the citadel. The weight that I carried, it returned slowly, an anchor to hold me down in the darkness that I called home. I think, along with the ocean and the peace, I liked this edge of the world so much because the shadows that were just lingering on the horizon felt like they understood what it was like to be me...

Shaking myself from my melancholy, I took one last look at the picturesque ocean and stepped off the edge of the cliff. The wind slapped into me as I descended, freefalling, and a burst of laughter rippled from me, sounding so foreign.

It had been a time since I had been able to laugh.

As I plummeted toward the jagged rocks, I sucked in a deep breath and smiled.

Wings of khaki and black snapped out from my back, the wind catching them as I beat them hard against the pull of gravity. My wings moved up and down, hovering me inches from the water below as another wave curled, rising up, ready to come again for the cliffside, but this time, I was standing in its path.

The wave rushed toward me, and I waited until the last possible moment before I flapped my wings and soared *upward into the skyline. I laughed again, knowing that when I played chicken with the waves, it was the closest I could feel to being mortal again.*

I lingered in the sky, flapping my unique coloured wings for a couple of heartbeats before I shifted my course and began to fly back toward the citadel, my heart becoming heavier with every mile I flew.

Movement to my right snared my attention and I glanced over to see feathers slowly falling from my wings. The moment they began to shed from the wings I had come to adore so much, they floated to the ground below.

I halted my flight, a wave of terror lodged in my throat as one by one, the khaki and black feathers melted from my wings, leaving nothing but musculature and skin. That too started to wither, to die, crumbling to ash as I cried out, because their loss, this pain that was suddenly spearing me in the chest, felt like I was losing a part of me that could never be regained.

Without my wings to keep me in the sky, I began to fall, to plummet to the ground below and while I mourned the loss of my wings, I was not afraid of dying. I watched as the ground appeared closer and closer still and I closed my eyes to blunt the impact as death reached out with her hand and yanked me to her embrace.

"She's convulsing again. Adair do fucking something."

A booted foot kicked me in the abdomen, and I let loose a moan as I pushed up on my arms to try and see who was attacking me, and yet, another swift kick to the stomach forced me to roll over on to my back. I tried to inhale some air, pain rippling through my chest.

"Let me just shoot her now. One arrow through the chest should do it."

My eyes snapped open at the familiar voice, my heart breaking as I looked into the handsome scarred face of the man who had been my brother since we were children.

"James..." I breathed out, his name nothing more than a whisper.

His lips curved into a snarl. "Don't. Don't fucking say my name like you know me. You lied to me, to us. A fucking monster. You were one of them all along."

I managed to get myself up and into a seated position, pressed my hand to my chest. "I'm sorry. I didn't want to lie. I'm not one of them. I'm still me. I'm still Raven."

James shook his head, looking away as he kept his crossbow trained firmly on me. I knew he could fire that weapon without looking at me again and pierce through my heart. It would shatter so easily, already cracked from the way James had looked at me, with hatred instead of love.

"We need to know what she told them, what she told him. We can't kill her just yet."

Tears slipped from my eyes as I looked over to see Tiernan watching me. His jaw was clenched so tight that it had to be painful, and his eyes were dark, his blue eyes almost navy as he looked over me and shook his head.

Tiernan looked ever the leader, a sternness replacing the man I knew who smiled easily and called me Trouble. He studied me like we had once studied traitors, right before we put a bullet in their heads.

"I didn't tell them anything. I swear. You don't have to do this."

"How does it feel, Raven, to have your death be at the hands of the person you love the most in this fucked up world?"

I cringed away from that voice as Hayes stepped out of the shadows, his eyes lifeless and the claw marks at his throat were now festered and rotted. Skin peeled from him, the scent of rotten flesh making me gag. I tried to look away from him, from them all, but I could not hide from the pain gnawing at my insides.

"She's afraid. I can see it. She's in a room with two human males, and fuck, she's terrified. She's so fucking scared. Not to die, no, that they stopped loving her. The dead boy is there too, taunting her. Her fear is pungent. Fuck!"

"What just happened, V?"

"She kicked me out of her head. She pushed me out so I couldn't see her fears."

I hear them taking about me, around me in a place I want to return to. Hayes' smile haunted me as he came over and crouched down in front of me.

"You will lose everyone who you love. Nature over nurture. Monster over human. It got me killed. It got Noelle killed. It will kill us all, in the end. Abomination."

I shift my gaze to Tiernan as he repeated Hayes' words. "Abomination."

A sob escaped my lips, and I crawled toward Tieran. "Please, Tiernan. Not you too. Please. I love you. Please don't turn your back on me."

There was a flash of confliction in his expression before he looked away from me, and I watched as he withdrew a pistol from at his waist, flicked off the safety and raised it so that it was poised and pointed right between my eyes.

I went to my knees, holding a hand over what remained of my tattered heart and pleaded for the man who had been my brother, my very best friend to forgive me. Our eyes clashed, held firm, and I saw the regret in his eyes a moment before he pulled the trigger.

"Raven, come on. Heal dammit."

I was running.

I was running for my life.

My lungs burned as I ran but I knew that running was the only way to stay alive.

My bare feet slapped against the stone as I bolted through the never-ending corridors of the citadel. Thunder rolled outside, followed by the deafening crack of lightning that speared through the darkened skies. The wind seemed to be in a frenzy tonight also, whipping my hair against my face, hard enough to cut. I scented blood in the air and knew it was my own.

And more of my blood would spill this night.

The sleepshirt I wore didn't shield me from the elements, nor did my exertion heat the blood in my veins. I was cold, so fucking cold. Terror was a hard fist in my stomach. A clap of thunder startled me and I stumbled over my feet, slamming hard into the wall and I felt something tear in my shoulder.

Once I had a grasp of myself again, I ducked down a narrow pathway, having to turn sideways to fit through and found myself in the dungeons. I couldn't be captured down here, for if I was, they would surely chain me up and yank the chain every time that they needed my abilities.

I hurried up the stone steps with no finesse or coordination, using my hands as well as my feet to ascend. Bursting out of the door, I paused to get my bearings, trying to clear the panic from my mind so that I could figure out how to escape the monster who stalked me.

My heart was beating so loudly inside my chest, I was sure that the monster could hear me and track me that way. Was it thrilled by my fear? Did it enjoy the hunt as much as it seemed to?

I heard a snarl of impatience and took off down the hall, not daring to chance looking over my shoulder to see just how quickly the monster hunted me. I could feel its presence, like a warm breath on the nape of my neck, ready to capture its prey.

Heading back in the direction of the place where the chase had begun, I burst through the doors of the courtyard, into the wind and rain, trying to locate a weapon to defend myself. The rain pelted down on me, soaking my skin, leaving my hair sodden and loose around my shoulders, sticking to flesh. I wiped the hair from my eyes, my heart sinking at the lack of weaponry in the training area.

It was as if I had been herded into a space that I knew down to my marrow, had hoped would help me against the monster, but I stood alone, defenceless and marked for death.

Something landed by my feet, and I looked down to see a feather of blue and white lying in a puddle. Then as I lifted my gaze to the skies, feathers of all colours, of all sizes and textures fell from the sky in tandem with the rain. I twirled around as the feathers drifted to the ground, falling softly around me.

Angels beat their wings, fighting a battle in the sky, faction against faction, League against Seraphan. The cries of war were as loud as the thunder that boomed and the lightening that pierced through the sky. It was devastatingly beautiful, the flash frame of the images and had I been artistic, I might have wanted to paint it from memory, immortalized for all to see.

The doors to the courtyard shattered, glass and wood splintering and I had to duck to avoid being impaled by a fragment. I braced myself for attack, knowing that against this creature, I'd never be able to fight it off. But I would not go down easy. I was ready for war and war had come banging on my door.

"Nathaniel...please.... don't..." I mumbled, and in that moment, I knew I was dreaming, that everything was just a nightmare.

"Raven? Raven? Fight dammit."

"I don't want to die," I whimpered, then slipped back into unconsciousness.

The monster loomed in the doorway; its eyes trained on me. A vicious snarl curled its lips, flashing me teeth. Its hands were clenched into fists, and I wondered if it uncoiled them, would claws be there in place of fingers that had once touched me with a tenderness that had made me ache?

"You lied to me!" It roared; the sound of his indignation almost drowned out by the rumble of thunder.

"I had to." I admitted to it, hoping that somewhere deep

inside, the monster might understand why I had to keep my secrets.

Reaching behind its back, the creature withdrew a sword, the metal becoming alight with flames. It was then that I could make out its features, even now, moments before my death, I was struck by how breathtakingly beautiful the monster from my nightmares was.

His inky black hair glistened with dampness, his storm-filled eyes raging as much as the storm around us. Sharp cheekbones and a chiselled jaw that I knew felt scratching to touch. His chest was bare, the mark of his rebellion on show for all to see. I had thought that he might understand that he might sympathize with my plight, with my curse, but the moment he realized that I had lied, I saw my death in his eyes and there was no way to talk myself out of it.

The flames on his sword danced a hungry dance, like they hungered for the taste of my flesh and were eager to sate that hunger. I looked from right to left, looked for a chance at survival, for a friend to come to my aid and save me from certain death.

But I was alone...there was no one coming to save me... and I could not save myself this time.

"I know what you are."

Frost in his tone, I shifted my gaze back to Nathaniel, my shoulders slumped. "I know."

Between one breath and the next, Nathaniel stood before me, the heat of his flames almost scorching my skin, but it was the heat of his gaze that threatened to burn me from the inside out. His free hand reached out and gripped my chin with a bruising grasp so I couldn't look away.

"I want to hear you say it. I want to hear it from your own lips. What are you, Raven?"

For a moment, it seemed like the entire world fell away and it was just me and Nathaniel left, not even the weather dared to interfere as I wet my lips and told him. "I'm a Nephilim. I'm half angel."

He growled at me, the fingers on my chin tightening. "A filthy half-breed with deceit in her blood. You fooled us all, Raven. And now I will put an end to your pitiful existence. And if you needed any proof as to why we are monsters, this will surely be enough..."

I screamed out into the real world, thrashing against what I knew was coming, the nightmare that haunted me over and over, knowing that my lies, my secrets would be the end of me. Hands gripped my shoulders, trying to hold me in place as I heard someone tell me that everything was alright, that I would be alright.

Nathaniel shoved me away, angling his sword a second before he struck, the blade going into my abdomen, but I felt it in the fragments of my heart. Fire licked at my flesh, the pain searing me as I went down on my knees, my eyes never leaving Nathaniel's as my flesh burnt and he raised the sword, one final swing at my neck...

EIGHTEEN

I came awake slowly, pried my eyes open. The room shrouded in darkness, the only light coming from the open window. It was enough to let my eyes adjust to the dimness. My mouth was dry, my muscles were sore, and I felt like I've been in one hell of a fight. I shivered from a chill that was set deep inside my bones.

Everything that happened comes back to me in a rush. The party, dancing with Nathaniel. Hayes dying. Aoife almost dying. I waited for the pain of losing Hayes to overwhelm me, but I was numb, I just didn't feel it.

I knew he would get himself killed if he came back to the citadel. I fucking knew it. He was so blinded by what he thought he felt for me, his jealousy, that he had to try and plot to kill Nathaniel, like I'd fall back into his bed if he managed to kill Nathaniel. Maybe I was being harsh, but Hayes wasn't cut out for this world.

It was something my mother might have said...fuck now I sounded like her.

My muscles ached and I stretched, my leg brushing against something toasty warm that made me want to curl my body into it. Turning my head, I froze at the sight of Nathaniel laying beside me in the bed. His eyes were closed, his chest rising and falling. His hands were clasped over his bare chest, and I wondered how long he had been beside me in bed.

I could smell the sweat and blood on my skin, and I wanted a shower so bad to wash it all off. Slipping from the bed, I tried to test to see if I could pull my power around me and got nothing. There wasn't a sliver of it inside me and for the first time that I could remember, I was powerless in more ways than one.

Shaking my head, I walked quietly to the door of the bathroom, pausing to glance over my shoulder. My eyes clashed with grey storm clouds as Nathaniel stared after me, some strange expression on his face.

"I'm just gonna take a shower. Go back to sleep. I'm okay."

I waited a moment to see if he would argue with me, however he just closed his eyes and angled his head away to stare at the ceiling. With a sigh, I walked into the bathroom, turned on the water and stripped off my clothes. My skin was even paler than usual, the dark circles under my eyes making me look haggard.

Stepping under the spray, I hissed as the water hit my skin, then just stood under it as I opened myself up to what had happened.

"She's telling the truth. She doesn't care about me. Not in

any way that matters. Hurting me to get to her won't work. It's a waste of your time."

I heard the pain in his voice as he said those words, truly believing everything he had said. I did care about him, just not the way Hayes wanted me to. Rieka jerked his head back and ran her tongue up the length of his throat. I wanted to fucking punch her so bad, but I couldn't make a move to stop her.

"Perhaps I should give him to Jophiel also. He is unique looking enough to make some decent coin, since you don't care about him, not in the slightest." Rieka kissed Hayes before continuing. "He tastes like rebel scum..."

Her words were said in a hateful snarl as she broke the kiss and having dug her nails into his flesh, I saw blood dripping as Rieka said with a smirk, her eyes now latched on me. "Don't you, Michael? Or should I call you Hayes now that we are well acquainted."

I should have known in that moment what Rieka's intentions were.

"Childhood friends, are you not? It would make sense as you are both similar in age and that accent is unmistakable. You thought you could hide from me, work an angle, and try and follow through on a plan to poison my son?"

I should have known she wouldn't let him live for having the audacity to scheme to murder her son. When Hayes bowed his head in defeat, I wanted to yell at him to fight, to be a soldier, to show them no mercy, but then Rieka is calling Makata forward.

A ripple of power filled the room as Rieka rested a hand on Makata's shoulder. I'm almost floored by the sorrow in

Makata's eyes, Rieka's hand changing into claws. I don't think I'm breathing. I don't think my heart is still functioning.

Hayes' eyes find mine. The smile he gave me was sad. Then he said. "It's okay. I love you. It's okay."

I should have lied. I should have reached into the pit of my soul and latched onto the sliver of humanity I had inside me and told him that I loved him back. I should have pretended, because he was going to die, and I could have offered him something to take him wherever we went when we died.

I screamed as Rieka's clawed hand swiped across Hayes' throat. Blood flowed from the wound and then Hayes is on the ground, dead, his lifeless eyes looking at me.

I heard Rieka say to me as she cleaned my friend's blood from her hand. "I always win, Raven. In the end, I always win."

I couldn't save him...I couldn't save him... There's nothing I could do to save him. Nothing.

"You look at him like you've never looked at me. He touches you and you give him this look that I've never seen before. How can you let him touch you when, after all we've been through, you flinch when I look at you. You have to know that I'm in love with you, Raven."

Words Hayes spoke to me when he'd confronted me about Nathaniel.

"It's okay. I love you. It's okay."

It wasn't okay...It wasn't okay.

"She doesn't care about me. Not in any way that matters. Hurting me to get to her won't work. It's a waste of your time."

He died knowing I didn't love him, thinking I didn't care about him.

"You have to know that I'm in love with you, Raven."

I had used him and discarded him, and my actions brought us here, not Hayes.

"You have to know that I'm in love with you, Raven."

It was my fault...all my fucking fault.

"It's okay. I love you. It's okay."

I could feel myself crying, and I heard the sob that escaped my lips, but I couldn't feel any of it. I should feel sad, I should feel something to go with the tears and the grief, right? Was this the confirmation I'd always wanted to know that I am as much of a monster as Rieka was?

Turning off the shower, I wrapped a towel around me, going to the toilet and then I towel dried my hair. Going back outside, I grabbed a pair of underwear and a t-shirt, pulling it over my head as I slipped back into the bed.

I laid my head down on the pillow, facing Nathaniel as he slept. While I was in the shower, he'd shifted to his side, and my heartrate quickened. It made me feel even worse that being near an angel who was my mortal enemy made me feel things, and the death of one of my oldest friends just felt sad, like any other soldier that had died.

A strand of dark hair fell over Nathaniel's face, and before I could stop myself, I reached out and brushed it away. When he didn't wake and call me out for my actions, I traced my fingers down the side of his face, trailing across his strong jaw and firm lips.

I thought back to the woods, after the angels had come to Cork to collect me and the way Nathaniel had kissed me. It had been hot, hard, possessive and it had consumed me.

I wanted to be consumed again.

My palm now travelled from the curve of his thick neck to his broad shoulders, his bare chest, along his sternum to the taut muscles on his abdomen. Feeling brave or perhaps foolish, I scoot closer to the heat of Nathaniel, his skin like a warm fire and I shivered.

I trailed my hand back up his chest, resting it over the handprint burned into his flesh. I'm reminded of what Verena told me about how Nathaniel was once a shy soldier, how Ascian had used his grief to manipulate Nathaniel to his way of thinking. I think of the angel who had written those journals, and the words I had said to him.

"When the man who wrote in that book wants to come and have a word with me, come see me."

Madness must have overtaken me because I leaned in and pressed a kiss to the handprint. I traced the outline of it with my fingers, dancing with danger as I felt Nathaniel tense and when I lifted my gaze to his eyes, I had a split second to brace before he growled, grabbed my wrist.

Between one breath and the next, I was straddling Nathaniel's waist, his hands on my hips, and then he was kissing me. I kissed him back, sliding my hands into his hair, scraping my nails against his scalp and the vibration from his growl had my toes curling.

He plundered his tongue into my mouth, tasting, sucking, licking, taking control, and showing me just how dominant he was. I was so used to being in control, the prospect of not being the one to take the lead was intoxicating.

Nathaniel sat up, and I wrapped my arms around his neck to stop from falling back. His black eyes looked like pure obsidian, flickers of orange as he broke the kiss, and just looked at me like he wanted to take a bite out of me.

"You were dying...you were dying in my arms and I... I ... there was nothing I could fucking do." Nathaniel said, his tone thick with emotion as he cupped my cheek, and I leaned into his touch.

I ran my fingers up and down the back of his neck. "I heard your voice. Even when I was dreaming, I still heard you telling me to fight."

"First goddamn time you ever listened to me."

I snorted out a laugh, rolling my eyes. "Well, just don't get used to it. Technically I was unconscious so I couldn't do anything but listen."

"Nathaniel, kill her."

"No. I will not."

"You defy me? For her?" I heard Rieka say sounding *utterly taken aback.*

"Yes, for her, I would."

"Will she punish you for defying her?"

"She can try." Nathaniel replied in an even tone, one that promised bloodshed and it was strangely arousing.

"I arranged for the human to be taken to one of the Rebel outposts."

Closing my eyes, I was relieved to hear that Hayes would go home to be mourned, and yet, I didn't want to hear about him now, even as Nathaniel continued.

"The boy, he loved you. He was the human you slept with the night before you came to the citadel to kill The Imperium. That's why he aimed a bolt gun at me in Cork."

Nathaniel wasn't asking me a question, just telling me what he had figured out. He waited, expectantly for an answer. Shaking my head, I went to pull back, but Nathaniel's hands snapped out to grip my hips, forcing me to stay where I was, but not so much that I couldn't have gotten away if I had wanted to.

"I don't wanna talk about him."

Nathaniel arched a brow. "Then what do you want?"

I wanted him...I wanted Nathaniel.

Desire shot through me, and Nathaniel inhaled, his nostrils flaring. "Raven, you need time to recover...you've been out for days."

In one way, I knew Nathaniel was being admirable, chivalrous maybe, and yet, I didn't want him to be worried that I had almost died again. I wanted him to want me as much as my body and heart wanted him. I wanted the passion, I wanted the intensity, and I wanted to pretend for a while that this thing between us wouldn't kill us in the end.

Moving my hands down his shoulders, I brushed my fingers over the arch of Nathaniel's wings, heard him swear, and that brought a smile to my face. I continued the motion, felt the feathers shift upward into my touch.

Leaning into the curve of his neck, I pressed my lips to his pulse, felt it jump as I flicked my tongue over it.

Nathaniel's hand was suddenly on the nape of my neck, pulling me back. He rested his head against my forehead, and I'm reminded of what he said to me in the forest, that he hadn't wanted to fuck me against a tree because he wanted to take his time with me.

Was he gonna put a stop to this?

"Don't reject me, Nate," I whispered into the silence surrounding us. "Not today. If you want me, then take me. *Please.*"

It's the please that gets him, I know, because I would never ask him for anything unless I really had to and now, I'm asking him to give us both what we have wanted, maybe since the first time we met.

His mouth slammed onto mine, and I can only ride the intensity of it, Nathaniel nipping at my lip for me to open for him and then he devoured me in a way that had my body igniting. I tried to kiss him back, grabbing hold of him, trying to close the gap between us.

Nathaniel flipped us so that I was underneath him, his large body caging me. I shivered as he pulled my tee over my head and tossed it aside. Then his mouth was on my skin, starting on my lips, then my cheek, before he blazed as he kissed his way down my body. He licked between my breasts and my breath hitched, heat drenching me between my legs.

I can feel the hardness of his erection against my stomach, and when I reached between us to get him to hurry the fuck up, Nathaniel grabbed my wrists and shook his head. "I told you I wanted to take my time with you. I want to lick and suck and taste you until you are wet and eager to take me into your body. I know that you have not experienced this properly so let me ensure that you are ready. Let me make sure that I can please you."

Not giving me a chance to respond, Nathaniel lowers his mouth to my breast and sucked at my nipple, making me arch into him. Sucking even harder, he flicked his tongue over the sensitive nub and that had me snapping my hands out to grip the sheets. He turned his attention to my other breast, using his mouth on that one, but his fingers pinched and rolled my other nipple.

If he continued doing that I was gonna come, just like I had in the woods.

Nathaniel smirked as he lifted his head. "You like having me at your breast. I'll remember that for next time."

I opened my mouth to tell him that this was a one-time thing and there wouldn't be a next time, but I'm left unable to speak as Nathaniel's lips move away from my breasts, moving lower, until he is lifting my hips and removing my shorts, leaving me naked beneath him.

I suddenly feel a little self-conscious. Nathaniel has lived a long time and probably had angelic beauties sharing his bed and then there's me, scarred and nothing to look at compared to other angels. My body tensed and Nathaniel lifted his eyes to mine. As if he sensed what I was thinking, with a smug smile, he parted my legs, and a lick of embarrassment flushed my cheeks.

"Fucking beautiful. I've fantasied about having you

come on my tongue since the moment you first gave me attitude."

His hands gripped my thighs, and then he yanked me to him, a yelp tumbling from my lips that was swiftly turned to a moan as Nathaniel licked at my core. He repeated the motion, his groan sounding pure erotic. Then he devoured my pussy with the same fever he had my mouth, using tongue and teeth.

As he moved his tongue in and out, I lifted my hips, greedy for him to go deeper. My skin was on fire, pleasure building like an inferno inside me as I ground my core against Nathaniel's face. It felt wanton, it felt so fucking right and my hand reached down to grip Nathaniel's hair.

"Oh god, Nate, I'm gonna...I can't..."

He chuckled against me, and I heard him mutter that was the point. I'm writhing now, trying to stop the pressure from building inside me, and I can feel the power inside me stir, and I'm worried that it will take me over again.

Nathaniel moved his mouth higher, then I feel one of his fingers at my entrance before he slid it in and I trembled. He stroked in and out a couple of times, testing me, and I'm on the edge, on the verge of eruption when Nathaniel lifted his head, looked me dead in the eyes.

"Come for me, Raven."

His mouth is between my legs again as I feel his fingers curl inside me, and it takes me over the edge. I screamed, the sensations so overwhelming. My body is shaking from the force of the orgasm as Nathaniel continued to suck at my clit and my eyes slammed shut as I rode the wave of pleasure.

Nathaniel eased me through it, and when I came back to myself, when the intensity ebbed a little, I lay panting and opened my eyes. The angel gave me a lazy, smug smile, his fingers running up and down my thigh. I would have told him to not look so smug, but after the rollercoaster of an orgasm, I hated that he had earned the right.

Nathaniel shifted up my body to kiss the side of my mouth, then he brushed the hair from my face, and I could feel the pulse of his cock against my stomach. "I liked having you come on my face, Raven Cassidy, Next time, you get to be on top."

CHAPTER
NINETEEN

My jaw dropped.

I must have looked absolutely scandalized because Nathaniel chuckled. "I think I like corrupting you in bed, Raven. Very much so."

My heart was still racing as Nathaniel ran a finger over my sensitive core, then sucked it in his mouth before he shifted off the bed. He looked at me for a hot moment, and I flicked my tongue over my lips as he yanked down his pants and freed himself.

I swallowed hard.

I knew it was a little morbid to compare Nathaniel to Hayes but my fumble with Hayes hadn't prepared me for what was about to happen. Nathaniel's dick was thick and long and had me wondering if the damn thing would fit inside me.

But his ego was already fucking sky high, so I wasn't about to tell him that.

Nathaniel crawled back onto the bed, his wings

flaring before he snapped them back in. He gently nudged my thighs apart again, and I shuddered, turning my head away. Nathaniel cupped my jaw and moved my head back around so that I had no choice but to look at him.

"Do you want me to stop?"

I'm shaking my head before he's even gotten the words out. "I'm not...I'm not sure I'm any good at this."

Nathaniel was trying to suppress a smile. "This?"

My cheeks felt like they were on fire. "Sex. I'm not sure I'm any good at it."

Nathaniel kissed me then, hot and wet before he pressed his hips forward, the head of his cock nudging against my slick pussy. "Can you feel how hard I am for you? How I'm always hard for you? You are beautiful and smart and sexy. We can have lots of practice until you feel like you are good at sex."

He gave me this sort of lopsided smile that had my heart skipping a beat, and I laughed out loud, rolling my eyes. Nathaniel's hands are tangled in my hair as he kisses me, his dick slowly pushing into me. I sucked in a breath as Nathaniel broke the kiss, burying his face in my neck as he murmurs. "So fucking tight. Fuck me."

Withdrawing just a little before he pushed in a little bit more, Nathaniel gripped my hips to stop me from wriggling, and I stop thinking about the pain, as my body adjusted, taking more and more of Nathaniel inside me with every thrust.

It's too slow. Too fucking slow and I'm impatient.

As Nathaniel withdrew his cock almost all the way, I

sense when he's about to enter me again, and I jerked my hips upward as he did, my nails scoring his back. Our pelvises bump when he slid into me all the way, and I feel it through my entire body.

Did you know that it was possible for an angel to break a human's pelvis with one hard thrust?

I flinched at the sound of Abraxas' voice in my head, and Nathaniel must have felt it, because he's looking at me. "Are you okay? Did I hurt you?"

I shook my head, not wanting to tell him that I was afraid that he might not only break my body, but shatter my heart too, because as much as I tried to deny it, I had feelings for Nathaniel. I knew here, in this moment, that he would not hurt me, and I gave myself to him freely.

"I'm okay. Just kiss me, okay?"

Nathaniel's kiss is softer this time around, though no less passionate. His hips started to move against, and I run my hands up and down his spine, my fingers grazing his wings. I can tell that he is holding back, afraid to hurt me and while it was nothing like I had ever felt before, I needed more. I wanted more.

I could feel the pleasure in my body shimmering, like it was waiting for more for me to be able to find release.

"Nate, I ...fuck..." I ground out as I tried to vocalize when I didn't understand my body wanted.

"Tell me, Raven. Tell me what you want of me. My body is yours."

I moaned at his words, committed them to memory. Sweat beaded on his forehead and I fucking knew he was holding back for me. I hooked my leg around his hip. "I need more. Faster. Harder. Just fuck me. Give me all of you."

Flames danced across his eyes as he held my gaze and then Nathaniel gave me what I asked for and all I could do was hold on as he slammed into me hard enough that the headboard banged against the wall. His hands slid under my ass to angle me and then when his cock thrust into me again, I could feel my power, and my ecstasy building.

Nathaniel's hips slammed into me, his mouth descended on mine as the waves crashed over me, the sound of his name swallowed by his kiss. And Nathaniel kept sliding in and out of me, as one crescendo surged into another and my walls clamped down around his cock.

His body was slick with sweat, and I was boneless, even as I felt Nathaniel's body tighten under my touch and then his cock was emptying inside me as he orgasmed. When he finally stopped, he leaned his head against mine, his chest heaving.

Nathaniel kissed me slow, tender and then he withdrew from me, making the aftershocks of my multiple orgasms make me let out a long moan. He moved off my body, rolling to the side and then he smiled at me, and like fuck if I didn't smile back at him.

"Okay you get to be smug for a couple of hours."

Nathaniel chuckled. "Only a couple of hours? Then I must not have fucked you enough if the sound of you moaning my name or you writhing against my face wasn't enough to earn me at least a day's worth of smugness."

Nathaniel grinned as I rolled my eyes, then pulled me into his arms. His hand travelled down my spine to rest on the curve of my ass, and I pressed into him, the heat of him, my leg curved over his hip.

"Don't get used to this. I'm not a cuddler."

I yawned, my head resting on Nathaniel's chest, and I can hear the beat of his heart in my ear. I feel the press of Nathaniel's lips on the top of my head and I let out a sigh. The duvet is pulled up over us, but I don't need it, because the heat of Nathaniel's body is enough to let me drift off.

When I wake, Nathaniel is sleeping beside me, and he looks less exhausted than he did when I first woke up after nearly dying. My power is back now, though it's kind of muted. I slipped out of Nathaniel's embrace, headed into the bathroom to pee, and gave myself a clean down below. I was sore, but not too much, and if I was being honest, I wouldn't mind a repeat of what happened again.

My stomach rumbled, making me snort and I quietly went back outside and pulled on some clothes, then slipped my feet into my boots. I went to the door, had my hand on the handle when I heard Nathaniel say my name.

I turned to see him looking at me from the bed, sleep in his eyes, hair all tumbled, and he looked sexy. "Go back to sleep. I'm gonna get some food."

Nathaniel closed his eyes. "Yes, food is a good idea. Then come back to bed so I can taste you some more."

Stepping outside as my cheeks heated, I closed the door behind me and leaned against it. I knew I was the one who had instigated last night, and things could never go back to how they were between me and Nathaniel before we had sex, and yet, I thought that this was always inevitable for the both of us.

Making my way to the kitchen, I kept my senses on alert in case anyone tried to kidnap or kill me again. When I made it to the kitchen without any incidents, I pushed open the door, surprised to see Adriel boiling water on the stove. His back was too me, but I knew from the way he held his shoulders that it was Adriel and not Adair.

"You'll have tea?" Adriel asked without looking back at me.

"Sure."

I pulled out one of the stools, and sat down, the slight ache making me blush as Adriel finished making the tea, turned, and set it down in front of me, pushing a jug of milk in my direction. I smiled in thanks, poured in the milk, then lifted the mug to my lips.

My stomach rumbled again. Adriel set bread and meat on the counter in front of me, then set a slice of chocolate cake down as well. I reached and pulled the cake toward me, breaking off a piece with my fingers and tossed it into my mouth.

"Mmmm, that's good." I mumbled around my

mouthful of cake, and Adriel shook his head, a rare smile curving his lips.

Adriel took his own mug and lifted it to his lips. Then he lifted himself up onto the counter next to the sink and just observed me as I ate. I was so fucking hungry that I devoured the cake, then half the bread and meat. I drank my tea and ate my food in silence, however when I finished, I let out a satisfied sigh.

"How's Adair?" I asked Adriel.

"Resting. He used up a lot of his power and now he needs rest to replenish it."

Tilting my head to the side, I set my mug down. "I never thought an angel's power could be depleted like that. Will he be okay?"

Adriel nodded, taking a sip of his drink before he replied. "In a day or two, he will be at full strength again. An angel's power is very much like a muscle. If you strain it, and then do not rest it, it can cause more strain. Adair healed the child, then Saskia, and then he had to heal you over and over when your heart stopped beating. Had you not stabilized before he passed out, then it is unlikely we would have been able to revive you."

Fuck...I was that close to staying dead?

"Would you have tried to heal me? If Adair couldn't?"

Adriel glanced away, and his shoulders dipped slightly. "You were at the very brink of death and my power; it didn't want to heal in this instance. It clawed at me to end your suffering. To take away your pain and claim your death as mine. There was not one spark of healing in me."

235

I don't know what to say to that, so I refrain from saying anything, picking at the crumbs on my plate and drinking my tea. Adriel grabbed a cake of some sort and tossed it at me. I caught it with one hand, and ate that too, unsure why I was so bloody hungry.

"You will try and kill her again."

I swallowed down the bite I'd just taken, washed it down with a slurp of tea. "I've never hidden the fact that I will keep trying to kill her."

Adriel's green eyes are steely as he replied. "Yes, we all know that you would kill her if the opportunity arose, but now that she has done something so brutal. That she has killed someone close to you and did so simply to score a point, I knew that you will wish to strike swiftly and enact your vengeance."

Draining the last of my tea, I hopped down off the stool to go and get myself another. "Call it vengeance if you want. I call it retribution. Hayes died because Rieka wanted to get one over on me. Show me up. She wanted to kill Aoife to prove a point. Rulers like Rieka, hell, even like my own mam, they will make you bleed and convince you that it's for the greater good."

Adriel waited until I poured myself another cup, fixed it up, and then went back to retake my seat. My friend said nothing in response to my words, so I just shrugged. "Can you seriously tell me that the majority of angels are happy with Rieka in charge?"

Adriel arched a brow. "If you kill her, then who would take her place? Nathaniel? Ascian? Is it not a case of better the devil you know?"

I shook my head. "No. There has to be a better way then all this bloodshed. There has to be more to this world than bitterness, oppression, and hatred."

"And killing the Imperium might just lead to the very war that you are trying to prevent."

"So, I just do nothing?" I asked Adriel, who shrugged, and I wondered what had gotten into him. "My sole goal when I came here in the first place was to kill her. If my life is sacrificed to achieve it, then I can die knowing my death meant something. Why are you arguing with me about this?"

Adriel set down his mug, then pushed off the counter to stand. "I am not arguing with you, Raven. I am merely asking you what you plan on doing next. Is killing Rieka more important and your death so insignificant that you would cause the people who care about you more grief?"

I'm not entirely sure who he's referring to, and Adriel sees it in my expression.

"Those human males you call brothers. Verena and Devika. Me. And the angel whose bed you just left, who's scent you wear on your skin. The people who care for you. Would you have us be the ones to kill you, knowing it would cause us pain?"

I'm a little angry now. I never wanted any of this ... I never wanted them to care about me.

"I didn't fucking ask you to care about me, Adriel. If you remember, I picked you to train me because you were the last angel I expected to want to be my friend. I'm not saying I'm not glad we are friends, but you can't toss that at me and expect me just to take it."

A muscle ticked in Adriel's jaw.

There was a pregnant pause the air thick with tension. I was just about to say fuck it and walk out before either of us said something we regretted when Adriel sighed, then said. "How do you kill a monster without becoming one yourself, Raven?"

I snorted. "It helps if you were a monster to begin with, I suppose."

This time, unlike many times before, Adriel doesn't argue with me when I called myself a monster, and it hurts like fucking hell that the angel I felt like I connected with the most was finally seeing who I was in truth, and that he might not actually accept me.

It fucking hurt like hell and this was why I didn't want to care for any of them.

Tears burned in my eyes, but I wasn't gonna let him see me cry. Fuck that shit.

Sliding off the stool, I turned away from Adriel and headed for the door. I waited for him to call out to me, to say sorry, or to talk through whatever had his knickers in a twist but he didn't. I opened the door, not bothering to look back as I whispered, knowing Adriel would still hear me.

"Yano, I never expected it to be you who gave up on me. Everyone else I wouldn't have been so surprised. But you. I would have sworn on my life that at the end, you would have my back. Sucks to be me, right? How did I get that so fucking wrong."

I walked out then, letting the door slam shut behind me and stormed back to my room, pissed off completely.

I stalked inside, snarling as I shut the door behind me and leaned against it, ignoring Nathaniel when he asked me what the matter was.

I didn't need to be thinking about the argument with Adriel right now. I needed not to be fucking thinking at all and Nathaniel could make me forget, even for a while. I kicked off my boots, ripped my tee over my head and got up on the bed.

When I could, I straddled Nathaniel and crashed my lips to his. Nathaniel's arm went around my waist, bringing my chest flush against his. I tried to deepen the kiss, but Nathaniel kept his lips closed and I pulled back to glare at him.

"Kiss me." I demanded, shivering when his hand went to my throat.

"Not when your anger is so evident I can taste it in your kiss. If you want angry sex, Raven, then you have it because I am the one who has angered you and not because you have had a quarrel with someone else. I will happily fuck the rage out of you when it is I who instilled it."

I'm ashamed of myself. I'm angry with myself and I shoved at Nathaniel before I clambered out of his lap and stalked away from him to pick up a glass from the table and tossed it at the wall with a snarl.

I kicked over a chair, then my hands clenched into fists, a scream lodged in my throat. Strong arms go around me from behind, and I tried to wretch away from Nathaniel, but he doesn't let me. He held my arms to my stomach, his chin resting on my shoulder.

Closing my eyes, I tried to gain control of my anger, and it slowly dissipates to be replaced with this sadness that might as well be tattooed onto my very soul.

If Adriel, who knew darkness as well as I did has rejected me, then what hope did I have that Tiernan and James might accept what I was? That Nathaniel might?

Nathaniel's breath was warm against my ear as he whispered. "Tell me what angers you, Raven."

CHAPTER
TWENTY

T he sound of a frantic knock on the door made me remember myself, and I stepped out of Nathaniel's arms as the knock sounded again. Shaking my head, I walked over and picked up the chair, righting it, as Nathaniel went and answered the door.

"I'm really fucking sorry to interrupt, but has Zephyr been here?"

The sound of panic in Devika's voice had me walking to the door and ducking under Nathaniel's arms. I ignored the way Dev's eyes flared when she looked from me to Nathaniel.

"What's going on?"

Devika ran a hand through her silver hair. "Zephyr heard about what happened to you and wanted to visit you. His mother told him not yet, and he was supposed to stay in his room and study while his mother went on patrol. I think he snuck out to come see you, but now no one can find him."

Fuck...Makata would lose her mind if she knew he was missing.

"He's probably hiding somewhere. We'll find him. Come on, I'll help you look."

Nathaniel cupped the back of my neck. "I'll get dressed and come find ye. Raven, put on your boots."

I rolled my eyes, although I did go back inside to put on my boots. I also grabbed the belt Nathaniel had given me, and turned to him, only to see him holding the axe out to me. Dev was still standing in the doorway as Nathaniel held on to the blade of the axe.

"We will finish our conversation later."

"Nope. We won't." I told him, but as I walked past, I halted and lifted my face toward him. The smile he gave me was brilliant, and the kiss, one that curled my toes.

I shoved Devika out of the way as she grinned at me, opened her mouth to remark, but I glared at her. "You can comment all you want after we find Zephyr. Come on."

We first went to the courtyard, where I knew Zephyr liked to hang out in the hopes one of the League would train with him. He wasn't there. Zeph wasn't in the kitchen or the library, and while Dev went to check on the school area, and the other angelic children, I went and checked the human quarters, doing so with my power pulled around me.

Still nothing.

When I came back up the stairs and saw Devika coming down the hall, I let go of my power, and shook my head when she arched a brow. Nathaniel came down the steps having gotten dressed, and Adriel was with him. When we didn't greet each other, Nathaniel looked from me to Adriel, understanding in his expression.

"Adriel, take Raven and go and check out the flight training ground. I'll rouse the rest of the League. The change in shift should be happening in less than an hour and Makata should not return to find that her son is missing."

I wanted to argue with Nathaniel, because I didn't want to be stuck with Adriel, but Zephyr was missing and that was all that mattered. I took off down the hall, jogging. Adriel could catch up with me if he wanted. I followed the path I'd memorized when Adair had brought me there the first time I'd met Zephyr, but when I emerged onto the ledge, there was nothing but the wind and rain to greet me.

Glancing upward, I checked the skies in case the young angel had taken flight, hoping to see him hovering above. I felt Adriel's presence behind me as I looked over the ledge and the drop made my stomach flip. I peered over my shoulder at Adriel.

"Here's your chance to get rid of me once and for all. One quick shove and I'd crack my skull open on the ground below."

Adriel frowned at me, as I shrugged, making to walk past him. His hand landed on my arm, and I looked him dead in the eyes as they blackened, then returned to their usual shade of green.

"I did not mean what I said. I did not mean to imply

that I had given up on you. I had something to say, and I relayed it wrong."

Adriel and I were so alike. It was the closest I would get in the way of an apology. It still hurt and maybe once we found Zephyr, me and Adriel could talk it out, but now, I would have to let it go.

"It's grand. We're grand. Let's find Zephyr. Our shit can wait."

We searched places in the citadel I had never seen before in my time here. Time ticked by and there was still no sign of the young angel. A sense of dread was now lodged in my stomach, and I knew that as more time ticked by that the chances of a good outcome was slipping through our fingers.

We gathered by the steps in the League quarters, me, Devika, Adriel, and Nathaniel. Adriel looked at Nathaniel. "We need Draegan. She can track him."

"She should be close by. Can we get her here without alerting Makata?"

Adriel looked at Devika. "Try and do just that. But if Makata is suspicious. Call everyone back. We should do that anyway. We need more help."

Dev nodded and bolted down toward the courtyard as I heard a voice behind me.

"I can help."

Slowly I turned to look at Saskia. She looked battered. Dark circles under her eyes, her hair pulled back in a severe braid. Her wings had started to grow back, and I could tell that it was painful. I shifted my gaze to Nathaniel, but he just lifted his shoulder barely, clearly deferring to me.

"Try anything, Sparkles, and I will gut you for real this time."

Saskia looked like she'd sucked on a lemon, but whatever retort she might have come back with was interrupted by the arrival of Draegan, Cassiopeia, Devika, Verena, and a very distraught looking Makata.

"She sensed something was wrong. They were already almost home when I flew out." Devika said, as Makata came up to Nathaniel. "I will not live if my son is gone."

Nathaniel embraced Makata. "Zephyr is strong. Resilient. You have trained him well. And we have no reason to believe he has come to any harm. Draegan?"

I had never seen the tracker angel's powers in full, but I watched as she closed her eyes, and simply breathed. She mumbled slightly and then her eyes snapped open, and she took off, leaving the rest of us to follow her.

I realized quick enough that Draegan was leading us toward the throne room. My stomach threatened to revolt at the thought of going back in there so soon after watching Hayes die, but there was nothing I could do except find out what had happened to Zephyr. If Rieka had anything to do with this, if she'd hurt the young angel, I would eviscerate her. I would rip out her cold dead heart and stomp on it.

Draegan flung open the doors to the throne room, and

we surged inside almost tripping over one another. My eyes scanned the room, as I heard Cassiopeia say Rieka's name and I had my axe out ready to cut the bitch. That was when I saw Rieka chained to a table, her head bleeding as she snarled and tried to free herself from the bindings. There was a gag in her mouth, and I couldn't help but feel a perverse pleasure at seeing her in such a state.

It would be so easy to go invisible and slit her throat. I would hold her under my power, so that Adair wouldn't be able to heal her. She would bleed out and that would be it.

I heard a laugh, a familiar one that haunted me, and I shoved through the angels to stand in front of a sobbing Makata. Abraxas was sat on the Imperium's throne, Zephyr on his knee where Abraxas had a gun pressed into his chest.

Where the fuck did Abraxas get a gun?

"Mom!" Zephyr exclaimed, tried to wriggle free but Abraxas tugged at the boy's hair, and tapped the gun against the child's chest.

"Zephyr!" Makata lunged forward, but Adriel caught her around the waist and hauled her back.

Nathaniel had his sword in his hand, the flames dancing up and down the blade. "What is the meaning of this, Abraxas? Let the child go!"

Abraxas laughed, rolling his eyes. "I don't have to pretend to take your orders anymore, *commander*."

The white-haired angel sneered as he said the word commander. I assessed the options in my head, was about to pull my power to me, when Abraxas shook his head and glared at me.

"Don't even think about it, Raven. The moment you go invisible, and I put a bullet in him."

I snarled, took a step forward, and poised with my axe. "What's the plan here, Abraxas? What leverage is a small child? You have the prize fucking pony chained up over there and you are holding a gun to a child? Fucking hell, Abraxas, you're dumb as fuck."

Abraxas growled, and I watched as he lifted the gun up and pointed it right at Zephyr's head. I could see from where I stood that the safety was off, and that his finger was poised on the trigger.

"I was just telling Zeph here that his auntie may have kidnapped him when he was younger, and Takara might have delivered the final blow to his father, but I was the one who drove a sword into his stomach and held him there so Takara could finish him off.

I can see that Zephyr is holding back his tears, and I'm proud of him for not letting Abraxas see that he had gotten to him. I'm not sure what Abraxas wanted to achieve here, but holding Zephyr hostage was not going to curry him any favours.

"What is this production all about, Abraxas?" Nathaniel stepped forward, sheathing his sword as he moved.

Abraxas tapped the gun on the side of Zephyr's head, and the young angel flinched. "I used to think the humans were more primitive than us. Less intelligent. Their weapons though? One bullet and Zephyr's brains would be all over the place. Adair is good but even he can't put brains back together. No healing the dead."

Out of the corner of my eye, I see that Verena has moved out of his line of sight and is making her way toward Abraxas while his attention is elsewhere. His head started to move toward where Verena was creeping, and I knew that in order for V to do her thing, Abraxas needed to stay distracted.

"So, Brax, what's your endgame here?" I started, moving to the right so that Abraxas' eyes would follow me, and keep his attention away from Verena. "You obviously have one since you waited for us all to figure out where Zephyr was. You coulda flown him out of the citadel while we were looking for him. Or killed him before any of us even realized he was missing. Come on, now, don't be shy Abraxas. You must be dying to tell us what this is all about."

Abraxas moved the gun away from Zephyr's head and pointed it at his chest again. Pale blue eyes watched me, as Abraxas smirked. "Deny it all you want, Raven, but you and me, we aren't too dissimilar. You have been living a lie for as long as I have. I've had to toe the line, take orders, and pretend that I was fucking sorry for my rebellion."

I kept walking along the right side, keeping my expression blank.

Abraxas glanced toward Rieka. "I endured having to fuck her, fuck Saskia, when all I wanted to do was carve their hearts out and eat them. But I did it because it was expected of me. And now that part is over with."

"You're Seraphan," I offered my conclusion not just to Abraxas, but to the entire League of Dominious in case they hadn't caught up yet. "You're Ascian's spy in the citadel."

Abraxas laughed, used the gun to point to the handprint on his throat. "Of course I'm fucking Seraphan. I've always been Seraphan. I pretended to be remorseful, to repent, and you fucking saps ate it all up. You lot think that you are safe here inside the walls of this fortress but I'm not the only Seraphan in the citadel."

I knew Abraxas usually talked a lot of shit, however, I had no doubt that Abraxas wasn't the only angel loyal to Ascian in the citadel. But what had changed? Why the hell was he revealing all this now, and risking death when he could have just said a massive fuck you to the League and fucked right off?

I clapped in a slow sarcastic applause. "Well, done, Brax. Well fucking done. Is that what you want? Someone to tell you you did a good job? What, does Ascian not stoke your ego and tell you that you're doing a good job? Good boy, sit, stay, fuck, betray like a nice lap dog?"

Abraxas growled and Verena slipped out from where she was hiding. Abraxas saw the movement, and before anyone had a chance to react, he fired a shot at Verena. It hit her in the stomach and Verena screamed in pain as she jerked, and staggered back to slide down the wall.

Devika surged forward as if to go to her girlfriend. Abraxas pointed the gun at Dev, and shook his head. "Ah, ah, ah, stay where you are Devika."

"Dev, it looks like there's a lot of blood, but Verena will be fine. It will hurt like a bitch but she won't die from it. Trust me."

Brax turned those pale eyes back to me. "Clever. Always so fucking clever. Trying to keep me distracted so I didn't see Verena sneaking up on me."

I shrugged, snorting. "Maybe I'm not very clever, Abraxas, maybe I'm just way smarter than you."

"Maybe we are both clever, Raven. And maybe we are both just the weapons our leaders made us to be."

I laughed at the audacity in his tone to compare us. "See that's where you are wrong, Abraxas. I was sent here because I was willing to die for the cause. You were sent here to be used as a fuckboy and scurry secrets to the Seraphan. I'm still actively working to kill that bitch and you had the opportunity to put your boss on the throne, but you couldn't follow through."

A muscle ticked in Abraxas' cheek. Then his gaze shifted from me to Nathaniel. "But you still ended up getting fucked too, didn't you Raven? And to think we could have ended up naked."

I probably should have dialled it back, considering that Abraxas still had a weapon on Zephyr. But I wanted Abraxas to focus on me, make a mistake, and then I'd kill him. I gave Abraxas a shrug of my shoulders. "I dunno, Brax. If I was gonna get fucked by an angel, then it sure as shit was never gonna be you." I glanced over my shoulder at Nathaniel, then back at Abraxas. "Having seen him naked, there sure as hell isn't any way I would be looking to get naked with you."

I'd obviously hit a nerve because Abraxas snarled and his hand holding the gun shook.

"Well, this is fun and all, but I've had a really long day and I'm exhausted so can we just move this along? Make your point already and let Zephyr go."

Abraxas pushed Zephyr into a standing position, one hand on the back of his neck, the other still clutching the gun. "I'll let the boy go. But I need something in return."

He was enjoying this. I could see it in his eyes. Abraxas was feeding off of everyone's fear, and pain, and liked having someone powerless. Just like when he tried to rape me, he got off on being the one who felt power.

"Are you waiting for me to ask what the hell it is that you want? For fuck sake, just spit it out already!"

"You!" Abraxas roared, the calm cocky exterior completely gone now. "This is all about you. Haven't you figured that out yet? The reason why Rieka is chained and gagged is because as much as I would like to kill her, I have no desire to be Imperium. And the only reason I've been called home, is because he wants you."

He? Like Ascian? What the fuck would he want with me?

I wanted answers to those questions, and yet, I was too stubborn to ask him.

"I took Zephyr because you are soft hearted when it comes to those you care about. You care about Zephyr and that means you will do what I want when I want. Everyone else is going to stay back. You'll walk toward Zephyr, and once you are up here with me, then I promise not to shoot the boy or anyone else."

"I'm making a counteroffer." I told Abraxas. "I'll trade places with Zephyr. You won't harm him anymore than you already have. I'll meet him in the middle and we both walk in the opposite direction then."

Abraxas snorted. "You hand that axe of yours off to Loverboy. Wouldn't want you getting any ideas."

I gave him a little shrug of my shoulders. "No hassle. It's not like I need it."

Taking the axe from the hook on my belt, I turned and walked back to Nathaniel, handed it to him. His hand landed over mine, and I looked into his eyes.

"You don't have to do this."

"I do. I really fucking do."

I could tell that Nathaniel was conflicted, that he didn't want me to offer myself to Abraxas but he knew that I would do it. Knew that when an innocent was involved, there was no way I couldn't not give Abraxas exactly what he wanted. The last thing I wanted to do was get up close and personal with Abraxas again. But I would do it. I would do it to save Zephyr. Even if it pained me. Because that was who I was, and it was what separated me from the likes of Abraxas, and of Rieka.

I cared too much even when I hated that I did.

So, I squared my shoulders and started walking toward Abraxas, a sense of dread dragging my feet as I walked.

TWENTY-ONE

I halted my advancement about a quarter of the way there, arching my brow at Abraxas, who had yet to let Zephyr go. He glared back at me and tapped the young angel on the chest with the gun. I stayed where I was, holding his gaze, then shrugged.

"You made a deal, Abraxas. Me for Zephyr. I'm holding up my end. You hold up yours."

Abraxas looked like he wanted to argue, but then he shoved Zephyr down the dais so abruptly the young angel stumbled before he found his balance. As soon as he started to walk toward me, I started to walk again, meeting him in the middle.

Zephyr's eyes were wide as he looked at me, this guilty expression on his face. He would blame himself for what was gonna happen to me when it wasn't his fault that we had ended up here. When Zephyr was about to stride past me, I stuck out my arm and made him wait.

"Tick tock, Raven. Get your ass up here or I swear I'll

start shooting. Verena's wound might not be bad but one in the head should do it."

"You can give me a minute," I snarled at Abraxas. "Just one fucking minute."

Ignoring Abraxas, I crouched down and looked at Zephyr dead in the eyes. His lips trembled and I could see he wanted to cry. I reached out and gripped his shoulder.

"It's okay, Zeph. It will be okay."

"I'm sorry, Raven. He told me he knew where you were. I didn't know he was Seraphan. I didn't know."

I gave Zephyr a small smile. "None of us did, Zeph. He had us all fooled." I lowered my voice, hoping he could hear me and no one else. "When you go back to your mam, tell her you need to stay and when I give you the signal, can you use your power to do exactly what we practiced?"

"I can try. What's the signal?"

"You'll know it when you see it." Because I wasn't sure what the fuck was gonna happen when I was in Abraxas' clutches.

I rose and ruffled Zephyr's hair. "Good lad. Now walk to your mam and give her a massive hug, okay? And don't worry about me. I'll be grand."

I made to walk away but Zephyr threw his arms around me and squeezed so hard that I was worried he might pop a rib. Then he untangled himself from me and started walking toward his mam. I lifted my head and continued to walk toward Abraxas.

The white winged angel was smirking, like he was the winner in all of this. I got to the end of the dais, then held up my hands in surrender. "What now, Abraxas? You gonna shoot me? I'm right here. Seems appropriate considering you don't have a power that can actually kill me."

Abraxas lifted his arm and pointed the gun at me.

I smirked and his hand trembled.

"Come closer, Raven. Come real close."

With a snort, I shook my head. "Hard pass. So, you do whatever was your end game here. Once I'm no longer leverage, they'll all tear ya about feather by feather. You remember how it felt, right? The scent of your burning flesh, the heat of it licking against your skin?"

Abraxas snarled and stalked down toward me. The moment he was within reach, I kicked out, catching his knee, and made to grab for the gun, but I misjudged his reflexes, and he was up and pointing the gun between my eyes.

I could tell that Abraxas was fuming as he reached out, grabbed my arm, and yanked me up on the dais. Spinning me around, Abraxas put one arm across my chest while the other held the gun, finger on the trigger. My heart started to race at the feel of Abraxas' body pressed against mine.

I stayed deathly still as Abraxas leaned in; his breath warm against the shell of my ear as he whispered. "I know what you are."

My heart skipped a beat and my eyes widened. No. There was no way that Abraxas could know what I was. He was saying something, anything to provoke me, to illicit a response and scare the shit out of me.

There was no way that he was about to spill my secret to the entire League and sign my death warrant... right?

Abraxas laughed, the sound so bitter and twisted that I shivered, closing my eyes as Abraxas leaned in again, and gave my ear a lick, bile creeping up my throat. I tried to reign in the rapid beating of my heart, to not give Abraxas an inch.

But I was fucking terrified.

Abraxas' lips travelled down to my neck, and I yelped when he bit down hard enough to break the skin. Nathaniel started forward, flames engulfing his arms but when Abraxas tightened his grip on me, I shook my head at Nathaniel.

I could tell that Abraxas was staring at Nathaniel as he licked at the blood from his bite, and could see the rage in Nathaniel's eyes. Adair and Asterin had joined the rest of the League, with Az readying a throwing star. Abraxas must have known she could hit him at this angle, so he made sure that I was firmly pressed against him, that on the off chance that Asterin did miss, she could end up hurting me.

"I always wondered how you could withstand so much and still function." Abraxas said, resting his chin on the top of my head. "At first, I thought it was the training you'd gotten from the Rebels. But I tortured another Rebel in one of the outposts and he broke, snapped like a twig, and spoiled my fun."

My pulse jumped as Abraxas ran the gun up and down my throat.

"Rieka let me try and break you. It made me hard, the anticipation of making you gasp with pain, and I swear to fuck when you did eventually scream, I almost came from the pleasure of it. That's when I decided I wanted to fuck you. To see how much rough you could take before you broke."

"That's enough, Abraxas." Nathaniel growled, fury in his eyes.

Abraxas laughed, then sniffed my hair and I wanted to vomit where I stood. "I heard you both, I heard her begging you- *I need more. Faster. Harder. Just fuck me.*"

Heat flared in my cheeks as Abraxas mocked me, and the thought of him listening to me and Nathaniel as we had sex made me feel dirty, exposed. Abraxas laughed again, the hand that was holding me on my shoulder, slipped down a little to graze against my cleavage.

"I don't know why no one even considered the possibility before..."

Anger snapped inside me. "For fuck sake, Abraxas, just fucking shoot me already and get it over with. Listening to you talk shite is worse than you torturing me. So, get on with it already and shoot me. Death would be better than listening to what you're saying."

Abraxas' arm lifted to hold me tightly as he snarled. "Our time is running out. But I think we still have a little time for the big reveal. Come on now, Raven. Tell them all, get it off your chest...tell them what you are."

I pressed my lips together in a firm line. There was no way in hell that I was going to out myself and put myself in danger because Abraxas was holding a gun to my head. I watched as the League began to spread out, and Abraxas' head turned to track their movements. They were taking up positions to strike and I couldn't help but cling to a little bit of hope that I could get free before Abraxas revealed the part of me that I never could tell a soul.

Abraxas fired a warning shot at the ground, making the angels stop. Then he pressed the warm muzzle against my skin, and I flinched at the heat. "Don't fucking move. Don't fucking move or the next one goes right into her head. Or maybe I'll just shoot V in the head."

For the first time, I looked over to see Verena clutching her stomach, her eyes filled with pain, but she was okay, which was the main thing. Adair attempted to go to her, however Abraxas fired the gun in the general direction of the healer, and then he took a step back toward the throne.

"Tell them, Raven. Tell them what you are before I put a bullet in one of your friends."

"Go fuck yourself, Abraxas. Go fuck yourself."

The angel holding me chuckled. "I'll tell them. I'll tell them how you've been lying to them all since the day you arrived in the citadel. I'll tell them all why the Rebels choose you to come, and not one of the other soldiers. If I tell them, they will all hate you...despise you like they do me."

"They'll hate me anyways." I murmured softly, closing my eyes, unable to stop the wave of defeat from crashing over me. The space between my shoulder blades burned.

"Tick tock, Raven. Tick fucking tock. Tell them."

"No." I snarled back at him, refusing to offer him this win.

The gun was pressed to the side of my temple. I kept my eyes fixed on a spot at the back of the room and exhaled slowly. This was it. This was the moment I died.

"Tell them, Raven, and then I'll tell them where they can find the broken bitch who I know you care about. Oh she tried to fight me, she tried to fight me right up until I told her that I liked it when she struggled. Then she went so still, I couldn't have taken her."

Oh god, oh no, Abraxas had Kalila...

"If you hurt her, I will fucking skin you alive, you sick son of a bitch!"

Abraxas just snickered at my threat. "Tick tock, Raven. I'm not sure how long an angel can breathe inside a box with no air. She's already been in there awhile."

Lifting my eyes to Nathaniel, pleading with him, I watched as he told Draegan and Cassiopeia to go, the two angels darting out of the room, and I knew Draegan would find her. But would they find her in time?

"They won't get to her in time, Raven." Abraxas sneered like he could read my mind. "She's going to die and that will be another person who died to keep your secrets. Tell me, did the human know what you were? Would he have still told you he loved you if he knew that you had been lying to him all this time?"

"I didn't lie." I ground out, hating how feeble I sounded.

"A lie by omission is still a lie. Tell them. Fucking tell them or I will. Kalila will die and it will be all your fault. They will still know but you will have more blood on your hands. Blood that you could have avoided!" Abraxas shouted at me, his voice loud in my ear.

I had no other choice.

This was the end of everything I held dear.

"I'm not human," I mumbled low under my breath, too low for anyone to hear me.

Abraxas jammed the gun into the wound where he had bitten me. "Louder! Fucking louder! It means nothing if they can't hear you!"

Something splintered inside of me and I screamed. "I'm not fucking human!"

The entire throne room went silent, confusion evident on the angels' faces even as I felt Abraxas press the gun in more, and I hissed. "I'm not human. I'm part angel."

I can see the shock on their faces, the revolution on some. Nathaniel is looking at me with this blank expression, cold and calculating, just like from my nightmares.

"A filthy half-breed with deceit in her blood. You fooled us all, Raven. And now I will put an end to your pitiful existence. And if you needed any proof as to why we are monsters, this will surely be enough..."

Tearing my eyes from Nathaniel, I glanced at Adriel, hoping I would not find the same look of disgust in his eyes as the other angels and to my surprise I saw only understanding, and not an ounce of shock.

Adriel had known. Adriel had known all along or at least suspected.

He had kept my secret...

I closed my eyes to shield myself from the pain of seeing the angels who had become friends look at me like the monster I was. Not entirely human, not entirely angel.

A half breed... a Nephilim.

"Raven."

My eyes snapped open at the sound of Nathaniel saying my name, but when he said no more, all I could utter in response was. "I'm sorry. I really fucking am."

Abraxas was laughing with delight now as he told them where he had hidden Kalila. On some level I was surprised that he had kept his word. I guess he was getting enough excitement from the pain he had caused me. Part of me was glad about that. Nathaniel ordered Saskia out of the room to go and tell the others exactly where Kalila was, and the sparkly bitch gave me a smug expression before she bolted from the room.

"Time's up, Raven. We need to be getting on our way."

"I'm not going anywhere with you."

"They will kill you," Abraxas said into my ear, and I can tell even the thought of it pleased him. "They will lock you up and pick you apart piece by piece to find out what parts are human and what parts are angelic. Adair will heal you, over and over until they get answers. I am your only hope of salvation."

Abraxas was fucking deluded if he thought that he was the hero in this part of the story. There were no heroes in this world, only villains, and those who did villainous things for the greater good.

The angel took a step back, toward the wall, and not toward any of the doors to the left of me. There was no way out for Abraxas behind us, nowhere for him to go. So, what was his plan here? I had no fucking clue.

But I'd take my chances with the devils I knew.

I waited half a heartbeat and then I sank my teeth into the arm Abraxas had across my chest. I bit down hard enough that I could taste Abraxas' blood in my mouth. I could feel his flesh tear under the force of it. Abraxas howled, and tried to pull his arm away, but I kept my teeth locked in place so his skin tore more until I finally felt his grip loosen.

I let go of his arm to spit his blood and flesh onto the ground, then grabbed for the gun. I'd taken him by surprise, but Abraxas still held onto the gun and I pushed the hand holding the gun downward, pressing my fingers over where his were on the trigger and used him to fire the gun.

The bullet went straight through his foot, and he roared in pain, dropping the gun. I pounced, kicking him in the balls, and when he lifted his eyes to mine, there was murder in them. My eyes darted to where the gun had fallen, and I dove for it.

Fingers grabbed my hair and yanked me backwards. I

spun, hoping to get in a blow or two, but Abraxas slapped me with the back of his hand hard enough that I felt something crack in my face.

Abraxas hauled me toward him, our faces mere inches from each other. "I can't kill you yet. But I'll send little fucking pieces of you back to Loverboy. Though I doubt he gives a shit about what happens to you now."

I hate to admit it, but Abraxas is right...

Abraxas hobbled toward the back wall, and then with a smirk on his face, I heard him call out. "Niran, now."

My heart stuttered. Niran- the angel who opened doors to other worlds and places.

My eyes landed on a swirl of black that suddenly started to grow in size. I struggled against Abraxas, trying to get away but he had a firm grip on me. There was no way I wanted to go into that black hole.

"Raven."

I angled myself to look at Nathaniel, who had taken a few steps toward the dais. There was a raging storm in his eyes, his body tense, and his shoulders rigid.

"I will come for you."

Fuck if I knew if that was a promise or a threat...

The doorway opened up fully and Abraxas shoved me forward. I elbowed backward, catching him in the stomach. Abraxas grunted, and as I tried to bolt. "Zephyr now!"

My axe appeared in my hand a moment later as I whirled and brought the axe down hard. Abraxas moved, the axe lodging in his shoulder as he yowled, he wrapped a bloody arm around my waist and hoisted me up, tossing me into the doorway.

There was nothing but cold as I moved from the throne room in the citadel to wherever Abraxas and Niran intended for me to go. I felt the darkness wrap around me, sinking into my flesh and bones.

Landing with a thud on the ground, I rolled over to my stomach and made to push up off the ground with my arms. A boot caught me in the stomach, and I collapsed back to the ground with a groan. My head was pounding, and I shivered as I spat blood out onto the ground.

"You stupid fucking bitch, you almost ruined it all!"

Abraxas kicked me again, my axe clattering to the ground too far out of reach, but I grabbed the foot I had shot and pressed the heel of my palm to his boot, forcing him to swear and back away, giving me a moment to catch my breath.

"I'll fucking kill you, you half-breed cunt!"

I laughed, then coughed and spat more blood onto the ground.

"You can try, motherfucker. You can sure as hell try."

A throaty laugh halted anything else I might have wanted to say to Abraxas. I pushed off the ground, kneeling as I brushed the hair from my face. My heartrate kicked up as an angel with gunmetal grey wings stepped out of the shadows and came toward me.

He had no shadow as he came to crouch down in front of me, his grey eyes clashing with mine. A bolt shot through my chest, and in that moment I knew. I knew before he spoke a word to me who this angel was.

Ascian, the leader of the Seraphan, gave me a warm smile. "Hello daughter. It's good to finally have you home."

The Story Will Continue In

ANGEL'S
SHADOW

WINGS OF DECEIT

BOOK 4

SUSAN HARRIS

PLAYLIST

<u>Angel's Traitor</u>

- Sam Tinnesz, Unsecret - We Need A Hero
- Story Of The Year - War
- Ruelle - Find You
- Manafest - Numb
- Halsey - Graveyard
- Fleurie - Breathe
- Wilkinson - Infinity (feat. ILIRA, iiola & Tom Cane)
- Collide - Wings Of Steel
- Collide - Halo
- Tommee Profitt - Cry Me A River
- Lansdowne - Halo
- Rain Paris - Pain // Happiness
- Ruelle - Where Do We Go From Here
- Muse - Uprising
- Tommee Profitt - Enemy - Sped Up
- Denmark + Winter - Do You Really Want To Hurt Me
- Rivals - Thunderstorm

- Ruelle - Secrets and Lies
- Koethe - Erased
- 2WEI - Strike & Rule (Prince of Persia)
- Pierce The Veil - King For A Day
- All Time Low - A Love Like War (feat. Vic Fuentes)
- Bad Omens - The Hell I Overcame
- Bad Omens - Malice
- YONAKA - Give Me My Halo
- PVRIS - HYPE ZOMBIES
- Zayde Wølf - Back in the Fight
- The Blue Stones - No Angels - TYRANTS Remix
- Sleep Token - Alkaline
- grandson - Identity
- Jarryd James - Do You Remember
- Vanic - Sacrifice
- The Band CAMINO - Last Man in the World
- Sam Tinnesz - Show You How It's Done
- Daughtry - Artificial
- Dylan - Liar Liar (Feat. Bastille)
- Paramore - Liar
- Ruelle - Yes We Can
- Royal Blood - Shiner In The Dark
- Stitched Up Heart - Conquer and Divide
- SATV Music - We Be Going Hard
- Tommee Profitt - Little Fight Left
- Tommee Profitt - Rise
- Tommee Profitt - Comeback
- Tommee Profitt - Secrets For Life

- Harpy - Inside Out
- Billie Eilish - bad guy
- Bring Me The Horizon - DArkSide
- Royal Blood · Pull Me Through
- Madalen Duke - Born Alone Die Alone
- VG LUCAS - Time's Running Out
- Bad Omens - Careful What You Wish For
- The Word Alive - One Of Us
- Bad Omens - Kingdom Of Cards
- Pendulum - Mercy Killing
- Written by Wolves - BURN
- Vansa - To Where You Are
- Pendulum - Halo
- AURORA - Your Blood
- EarlyRise - The Villain
- VUKOVI - MERCY KILL
- Lacey Sturm - Not Your Fight
- ONE OK ROCK - Make It Out Alive
- Mother Mother - The Matrix
- Spiritbox - Too Close / Too Late
- Amira Elfeky - Everything I Do Is For You
- Des Rocs - Used to the Darkness
- Dylan - Rebel Child
- Bad Omens - V.A.N
- Boston Manor - Halo

Also by Susan Harris

THE WINGS OF DECEIT SERIES

Angel's Gambit, book 1

Angel's Rebel, book 2

Angel's Traitor, book 3

Angel's Shadow, book 4

THE EVER CHACE CHRONICLES

Skin & Bones, book 1

Collateral Damage, book 2

Smoke & Mirrors, book 3

Night of the Hunter, book 4

Never Back Down, book 5

Shortcut to the Grave, book 6

Arsonist's Lullaby, book 7

Of Gods And Monsters, book 8

Shattered Memories

~

SICARIUS SECURITY

Kiss of Death, book 1

Leap of Faith, book 2

Visions of Destiny, book 3

War of Hearts, book 4

Flames of Conflict, book 5

DEFY THE STARS

A Tale of Two Houses, book 1

Until Death Do Us Part, book 2

In Defiance of the Stars, book 3

Courting Darkness, a novella

THE SANGUINE CROWN

Chaos Theory, book 1

Butterfly Effect, book 2

Wicked Game, book 3

Burn Notice, book 4

Fight Song, book 5

THE MURDERING HOUR NOVELS

Own The Night, book 1

Dwell In Darkness, Book 2

A Lot Like Christmas Anthology

The Rebel County Universe which will span eight different businesses, all intersecting with characters popping up when you least expect them.

THE REBEL RACERS TRILOGY

Available Now:

Adrenaline Junkie (Rebel Racers Book 1)

All or Nothing (Rebel Racers Book 2)

Crash and Burn (Rebel Racers Book 3)

THE REBEL ROCK TRILOGY

Available Now:

Centre Stage (Rebel Rock Book 1)

Strings Attached (Rebel Rock Book 2)

Make or Break (Rebel Rock Book 3)

THE REBEL INK TRILOGY

Available Now:

Breaking the Habit (Rebel Ink Book 1)

Uncomfortably Numb (Rebel Ink Book 2)

Secrets In Ink (Rebel Ink Book 3)

ACKNOWLEDGMENTS

None of this would be possible without an amazing team supporting me! Many thanks to:

Publishing House: CTP Publishing
Cover design: Gem Promotions
Interior Formating: Gem Promotions
Proof Reading: Ashley Brilinski

And as always:
Thank you to all the readers!
Whether this is your first book by me or you've been with me for years! I only get to do this because of you, and I am eternally grateful to each and every one of you who took a chance on this Irish author.

About the Author

Susan Harris is a writer from Cork, Ireland and when she's not torturing her readers with heart-wrenching plot twists or killer cliffhangers, she's probably getting some new book related ink, binging her latest TV or music obsession, or with her nose in a book.

Susan LOVES connecting with her fans!

Made in the USA
Columbia, SC
02 September 2024

41529406R00171